Cupid's Misfire

Hot Holidays Book 3

Ellis O. Day

I love to hear from readers so email me at
authorEllisOday@gmail.com

https://www.EllisODay.com

Follow me

Facebook
https://www.facebook.com/EllisODayRomanceAuthor/

Closed FB Group (sneak peeks, sample chapters, and other bonuses)
https://www.facebook.com/groups/153238782143373

Bookbub
https://www.bookbub.com/authors/Ellis-o-day

Instagram
https://www.instagram.com/authorEllisOday/

Twitter
https://twitter.com/Ellis_o_day

Join My Readers' Group and for a limited time get the entire Six Nights of Sin series for FREE
(THERE'S A PEEK OF BOOK ONE AT THE END OF THIS BOOK)

Join my newsletter to get your FREE books

Here's What You Get When You
Join My Readers' Group

Win Before You Can Buy
Exclusive Giveaways
Free Books
Sneak Peeks

CHAPTER 1: ADRIAN

Adrian helped Ellie carry her bags of clothes and other items up to his place. "We can get whatever else you want from the storage facility tomorrow."

"Oh, no. I won't need much. I won't be staying long." She stopped as soon as she entered the apartment, as if not sure where to go.

He walked around her and opened the door to the spare room, placing the bags on the floor near the door. "Not much but it's a place to sleep." It had a closet, a window, full-sized bed with a green comforter and a dresser. "My sisters sometimes crash here if they're in the city. They say the bed's comfortable."

"I'm sure it's great." She dropped her bag and purse on the dresser and turned toward him. "Thank you again."

"It's not a problem." He forced his eyes not to look at that bed. It was making his thoughts run in directions they shouldn't.

He'd never fucked on that bed. He'd never fucked in a lot of places in his apartment. He needed to remedy that. It didn't matter that he'd only recently moved here. It wasn't right for a man not to have fucked in every room of his apartment. It brought bad luck or something.

"Don't worry. I won't overstay my welcome. I'll start looking for an apartment right away."

"Ellie, I said it wasn't a problem and I mean it." He

was getting a little tired of her running as fast as she could in the other direction. "I never use this room or that bathroom. It's all yours." Shit. Now, he was thinking about the shower. She'd be wet and slippery. He'd have to hold on extra tight to keep her in place.

"Speaking of showers."

His dick perked to attention. Maybe they should start the no sex thing tomorrow…or never. He had no idea why he'd brought that up. Oh, that's right. His pride had been hurt. Fucking stupid pride. Now, it was his dick that hurt and that was so much worse than a ding to his feelings.

"Do you mind if I take one before I turn in for the night?"

"No, not at all. It's your place too." He dropped onto the couch. It was late but he wasn't tired enough to sleep.

She went into her bedroom and a few minutes later walked into the bathroom. She came right back out. "I didn't pack any towels. Do you have one that I can borrow?"

"Oh. Right. One minute." He headed for his room.

He kept hand towels in there but not bath towels. An image of Ellie trying to cover her luscious body with a tiny hand towel flashed in his head. He had to stop thinking like that or he was going to walk around with a permanent hard-on for the next few days.

He grabbed three towels and went back into the living room, handing them to her. "Anything else?" *Like him washing her back and other softer places.*

"Nope. Thanks." She held up a small bag. "Brought

2

my shampoo and other stuff from home." Her eyes dimmed on that last word and his desire shifted to concern.

"You can stay here as long as you want."

"Thank you." She smiled. It was soft and shy, another one for his memory book of Ellie's awesome smiles. She turned and closed the door behind her.

He should walk away but instead he stood there imagining her pulling her shirt over her head and then removing her bra. He could see those nipples now, puckering from the chill, waiting for his mouth to warm them. Her breasts would sway gently as she shimmied out of her pants and underwear before stepping into the shower. The water would cascade over her. She'd lift her hands above her head to wash her hair. Her breasts would tip upward, nipples hardening like he was sucking on them. His hand drifted to his pants, giving his cock a squeeze and wishing it was her hand or her mouth. Fuck.

He turned and headed for his bedroom. A shower was a good idea. She'd never hear him jerking off in there.

CHAPTER 2: ELLIE

The bed was comfortable, but Ellie couldn't sleep. Adrian was in the living room watching TV. She strained to hear what was on, anything to keep her mind from remembering that glance he'd given her when she'd come out of the bathroom. At first, she'd been sure it'd been desire in his eyes and her body had responded like Pavlov's dog. Then he'd grumbled goodnight before turning back toward the television.

Had he been disappointed that she'd been dressed in sweats and a T-shirt? She'd even put on a running bra because she wasn't going to walk around braless in front of him, even for the quick trip to her bedroom. Had he really meant the no sex thing? She wasn't going to have sex with him again but that didn't mean she didn't want to.

It was no use. She couldn't sleep. She hadn't thought to grab her ereader or any of her books. All she had was her phone and she was tired of playing games and scrolling through social media. She got up and walked into the living room. Adrian was stretched out on the couch.

"Hey." He sat up. "Is the TV too loud? I'll turn it down."

"No. It's fine. I just can't sleep."

"Oh." He scooted to the other side of the sofa. "You want to watch something? This is almost over. You can pick the next show." He gave her a cocky grin that made her want to wipe it off his face with kisses. "You can even pick a romance if you want but only because it's your first night here. After tonight, no romances."

"Really?" She sat, squeezing as far against the other side of the couch as she could. She even put a pillow on her stomach. She needed something to hold on to, so she didn't reach for him. "Then no sports."

"Damn. Okay. You can watch romances." He made a face like he'd eaten something rotten. "But no romance and no sports during shared TV time."

"You'll actually give up watching sports?" Even her father wouldn't do that.

"I grew up with six sisters. I'm used to it."

"Then you should be used to watching romances too."

He laughed. "No, because when they came on me and my dad would leave and do something else. The girls learned, with mom's help, not to pick romances when dad was home."

"He wasn't always home at night?" She wanted to know about his family. He spoke of them with such fondness and humor.

"He worked shift work, so no."

"And when he wasn't home, they watched romances

5

even though they knew you didn't like them?"

"They watched them *because* they knew I didn't like them." He chuckled. "But I got even. I'd sit in the living room, explaining how stupid the shows were. It annoyed the hell out of them."

She laughed. "Robbie, my brother, tried the same thing but Tina and I retaliated by telling his friends how he always had to be in the room whenever we watched some sappy show."

"You're mean."

She started to laugh but the humor fled when she recalled the last time, he'd said that to her. She'd had him tied to his bed.

He must've remembered it too because he cleared his throat and offered her the remote. "Your pick."

"You're letting me handle the remote?" She stared at it, flabbergasted. None of her other boyfriends had ever conceded control of the remote, even when they let her choose the show.

"You know how to use it, right?"

"Of course, I do."

"Then, yeah." He stood. "Want something to drink?" He walked into the kitchen and opened the fridge. "I have beer, water and one Coke."

"I'm trying to get sleepy, so water."

"Beer's a depressant."

"Sure. I guess." She'd already had a few at Murphy's but it wasn't like she was going to jump him after one more drink.

He handed her one of the two bottles he carried and dropped back onto the couch. "What are we watching?"

She scrolled through the guide. "Have you seen Mindhunter?"

"No. I've heard it's good." He glanced at her. "You like those kinds of shows?"

"I love them. Have you read John Douglas' books?"

"Read them? I own every one of them."

"Me too." She smiled and their gazes met and held. Her body swayed toward his. His lips were like a magnet drawing her closer.

He blinked, clearing his throat again and turning toward the TV. "Aren't you going to start the show?" He relaxed back against the couch, stretching out his long legs in front of him.

"Yeah. Right." She pressed the button and leaned back into her corner. Apparently, he'd been serious about the no sex thing. She was glad. Really, she was but he didn't have to look so comfortable about it.

CHAPTER 3: ADRIAN

"You need help bringing anything up?" Adrian asked as Ellie came into the apartment.

After staying up late and watching TV together he'd heard her moving around very early the next morning. She hadn't been loud, but he hadn't slept well. He'd kept trying to figure out a way he could convince her to join him in his bed and save his pride. Since he'd been the dumb fuck who'd made the no sex rule, he couldn't be the one to break it.

He'd offered to go to the storage facility with her, but she'd politely refused. He wasn't giving up. Watching television together was a start. He'd gotten her to promise not to watch Mindhunter without him which would force them to spend some time together. Now for the next step.

"No. I only picked up a few things." She dragged a large suitcase behind her.

"I see." He tried not to smile but she had to have heard the humor in his voice.

"It's not that much."

"If you say so." He stood and brushed her hand away.

"It looks heavy, let me."

"I can do it."

"I know you can, but I want to help." He lifted it. "Damn, what do you have in here bricks?"

"Books."

"Is it filled with them?" This thing weighed a ton.

"No. I have clothes in there too."

"My money is on more books than clothes." He carried it to her room and stopped at the door. "May I?"

"It's your apartment."

"It's your room. I was raised to never go into someone's room without asking first."

"That's a good rule but go right ahead."

"I used to think it was for my sisters' privacy but as I got older, I realized it was more for my parents. With seven kids they had to protect their alone-time."

"I don't even want to think about my parents and sex. I know they had sex but—"

"Had? I'm sure they still do." Sure? He was positive. Although he'd never seen them fuck on stage, there was no way the show they put on wasn't followed by a private performance of cock-in-pussy. He put the suitcase down on the bed.

"Yeah, I know and I'm happy for them but..." She made a face. "I'm happier not thinking about it."

"Okay. Then change of subject. You ready to go shopping or do you want to unpack the suit...your books first?"

"They aren't all books and I'll do that tonight."

"Then let's go get some groceries." His parents went to all the stores together now that their kids were raised. He'd asked his mom about it once and she'd said it made them closer. They had a great relationship and he'd take all the tips he could get.

CHAPTER 4: ADRIAN

Adrian followed Ellie around the grocery store as she pushed the cart. He tried not to stare at her ass but damn, he wanted to slap that thing or squeeze it. At this point, he didn't care which, but he had to keep his hands to himself and stay focused on his long-term goal.

"Peanut butter." He grabbed a jar from the shelf and then three jars of jelly—one strawberry, one apple and one orange.

"What are you ten?" She grinned at him. "I don't think I've eaten PB&J since grade school."

"You should try it. It's delicious." He wouldn't mind putting some peanut butter and jelly on her body and licking it off. *Focus, damn it*. He could make her his personal PB&J later, but hopefully, not too much later.

"I'll stick with my feta cheese, hummus and wraps."

"I make an awesome Greek Village Salad."

"Really? You cook?"

"Of course, I cook but there's no cooking involved with this." From the way she'd said that Marc must not have been much of a chef. Score one point for him. "Come on." He walked toward the aisle with the olives and pickles. "I'll make it for dinner Monday night."

"Why not tonight?"

"It's better if it sits overnight."

"Okay. I can make a Greek salad or gyros to go with it."

"Sounds good." This was working. His parents were right.

"What about tonight?" He moved closer to her and lowered his voice, "Promise not to tell anyone but I make an excellent vegetarian chili."

"Why would anyone care?"

"Vegetarian." He gave her an exasperated look. "I'd never hear the end of it from the guys."

She laughed. "I promise. I won't tell a soul."

"Then chili it is for tonight. Let's get the stuff."

By the time they made it to the produce section Adrian's cart was full of crap. He'd never known a woman to eat so much junk food. She'd grabbed potato chips, pretzels, Doritos and tortilla chips but those, according to her were for the nachos she was making later that week.

"Oh, popcorn." Ellie grabbed a bag from the produce section. "Do you have an air popper?"

"No. I buy the microwave stuff. I didn't even know they sold popcorn in the produce section." He grabbed a bag of apples.

She made a face. "Microwave popcorn smells good but

tastes gross. I'll go to the storage shed and get my air popper. We can have popcorn and soda when we watch Mindhunter. Oh…" She almost jumped with excitement. "We'll need lots of butter. I'll go back to the dairy section and get more." She stopped. "Is there any kind you prefer?"

"Whatever you like is fine." Today was looking up. Apparently, they were going to watch TV together again. It may not be much, but it was a start.

CHAPTER 5: ELLIE

Ellie trudged up the stairs to the apartment. She was beat but it was her night to cook. She'd been staying with Adrian for over a week and because of him she hadn't been sleeping well. She walked into the apartment.

"What's for dinner?" Adrian had obviously just gotten home from work too because he was still in his dress pants and polo shirt, instead of those blue jeans that hugged his ass and were slightly faded in the front. That spot always drew her eyes, making her remember exactly what he had hidden in there.

Damn, she missed sex. It'd been ten days since she'd moved in which meant ten days since she'd had sex. She'd gone longer but it was different with Adrian walking around in a constant state of undress. The man was always changing in front of her.

He took off his shirt and tossed it in the laundry basket. "You making that stir fry again?"

"Do you have to do that here? Your room is only a few feet away." She pretended to wipe her nose as she casually ran her hand over her mouth to make sure there was no drool dripping down her face.

"Do what?"

"Undress."

"Why? Does it bother you?" He stared at her, but she couldn't read his expression, probably because her eyes kept darting to his chest.

"No. Do whatever you want." She strode to her room, closing the door behind her and leaning on it. Damn, she wanted that man, and it was driving her crazy.

"Are you making stir fry?" he yelled from the living room.

"No." She wasn't ever coming out of this room again.

"Why not? We have the ingredients."

He had to stop referring to them as we because they were never going to be a couple. "I know what I have. I bought it."

"Okay. I was just asking."

She walked to her closet, taking deep breaths as she started to undress.

"What are you making?" His voice came from right outside the door.

She wanted to race across the room and fling the door open. Let him see her undress for once. Let him feel a tiny bit of her suffering. That was it. She removed the rest of her clothes and wrapped a towel around herself. "I'm not sure. I'm going to shower first." She opened the door, wearing nothing but that short towel.

His eyes locked on her cleavage and then traveled slowly down her body. His face hardened and she suddenly felt much happier. It was true. Misery did love company.

"Excuse me." She stepped past him, making sure her breast brushed his arm. She fought a grin at the slight intake of his breath. Oh, yeah, this was much, much better.

CHAPTER 6: ADRIAN

Adrian pulled into the parking lot at his apartment and took a moment to prepare himself before entering hell. The first week or so of living with Ellie had been torture but nothing he couldn't handle. Now, he walked around in a constant state of arousal and it was all her fault.

Instead of wearing big, baggy sweats and an even baggier T-shirt with her breasts strapped down so tight by some kind of running bra or torture device that they didn't even move, she pranced around the house in yoga pants and a spaghetti string tank top. He'd go to bed every night with his dick talking to his bellybutton and a headache from his eyes bouncing back and forth between her tits and her pussy. If he looked hard enough, he was pretty sure he could make out those pussy lips. Fuck, he wanted to kiss them again.

On top of all that torture, she seemed oblivious to him. She used to be nervous when he'd stand or sit too close and every now and then, he'd catch her staring liked she wanted to tear his clothes off and devour him. He'd prayed many times that she would. He wouldn't be breaking his rule if she made the first move. Actually, he'd be the bigger person by modifying his rule for her—in this case from no sex to sex all the fucking time.

He groaned and made his way to his apartment. He had an hour or so before she arrived. He could shower and jerk off just like every other fucking day. He opened the door and almost turned around. His nightmare had begun early.

Ellie sat on the couch in short shorts. He was pretty sure if she spread her legs, he'd be able to see the hair on her pussy. As a matter of fact, he'd see it up close because if she spread those legs, he'd be on her like a starving man.

"Hey." She smiled up at him.

Hell was super-hot today. He was going to bust a nut looking at her mouth. "Why are you home early?"

"Oh. Ah. My boss let me leave. We finished phase one of the project way ahead of schedule." She stood. "Are you hungry? I made dinner."

"Yeah." Hungry for her. "It smells great." He headed toward his bedroom, unhooking his tie.

"Where are you going?"

"To shower." And jerk off.

"I made sure everything would be ready when you got home. Fajitas aren't good cold." She stood by the kitchen doorway and he wanted to drop to his knees and lick his way up her legs. "Are you coming?"

His eyes snapped to hers. She had to be flirting but her expression was innocent. "Yeah. I'm coming." He would be as soon as he got in that shower.

He followed her into the kitchen, unfastening the top

buttons on his shirt. The kitchen was a fucking mess. He'd tried to teach her to clean as she cooked—finish using a pan, rinse it and load it in the dishwasher—but she refused.

He grabbed a beer from the fridge and sat at the table. "Looks good."

She had all the accoutrements—guacamole, salsa, tortilla chips, and warmed flour tortillas—spread out like a buffet.

"Thanks." She carried a hot pan filled with meat and vegetables to the table. She leaned down, her shirt gaping open, as she placed it on a trivet.

His throat dried like he'd eaten sand as he stared at her breasts. The bra she wore was lace and he could see her nipples, rosy and hard. He rubbed his hand on his leg to keep from reaching out and pinching those little nubs.

"Go ahead. Help yourself."

He started to raise his hand. She'd given him permission. He was fucking taking her up on her offer but then he looked at her face. She wasn't flirting or even looking at him. She sat and grabbed a flour tortilla, filling it with vegetables and meat from the pan.

He barely contained his snarl. She didn't even notice him anymore. A few weeks ago, if she'd made a comment like that, she would've been watching him with a mischievous gleam in her eyes. Now, the only thing she was interested in was the fucking food. He grabbed his beer and drank about half of it. He needed something to cool his erection or soon it'd be knocking on the table.

"Aren't you going to have any?" She smeared some

sour cream on her fajita and took a big bite. She chewed and swallowed, the motion of her throat making his dick get even harder. Then, she licked her lips before moving that rolled up tortilla back to her mouth and opening wide.

He couldn't pull his eyes away. He wanted her guiding his cock between those lips just like…He flinched when she took another big bite. Okay, not exactly like that.

"I picked up some more chicken nuggets too, if you'd rather them."

"What? No. This is good." He grabbed a tortilla and filled it, trying not to get the onions.

"Are you sure? If you don't like fajitas, I can heat up some nuggets."

"I like fajitas." He took a bite. It was good.

"Okay." She didn't sound like she believed him.

"Why do you think I don't like fajitas? I'm eating it right now." He wasn't thrilled with the condescending smirk teasing her lips.

"It's nothing."

"What?" He dropped the wrap onto his plate. He knew that look. His sisters used it every time they thought he was being an idiot about something.

"I…I don't want to fight. It's nothing."

"Tell me. Now."

"Okay." Her eyes met his across the table. "You eat like a ten-year-old." She stuffed the last of her fajita into her mouth.

"Me? I eat like a kid? What about you with all your chips?"

"I like snacks, but my meals consist of adult foods." She began making another fajita. "See. I even eat the vegetables."

"So do I." He took another bite of his tortilla.

"Please. I saw you trying to get as few vegetables as possible without actually tossing them back into the pan."

"I don't like them when they're really big but that doesn't mean I eat like a kid." A few weeks ago, she didn't consider him a child.

"Please. Your favorite foods are PB&J, bologna, chicken nuggets and hot dogs."

"I eat other foods." He finished his fajita wrap.

"Name one thing that you eat on a regular basis that children don't." She took a gulp of her water and then began eating her second fajita.

"Yogurt." He didn't have to tell her that it'd taken him years to learn to tolerate the semi-sour taste of it.

"Kids eat that all the time." She gave him a disgusted look.

"I drink beer." He picked up his bottle and finished it.

"Kids aren't allowed to drink beer, or they probably would."

"I don't think they'd like the taste." He walked to the refrigerator and grabbed another one.

"I guess we'll never know. So, it doesn't count."

"I eat salad all the time and that's almost all vegetables." He sat back down.

"You smother them in salad dressing like a child."

Maybe he did eat like a kid. His tastes were simple like

his life—work hard, play hard and take care of his family. Those were the rules he lived by and there was nothing wrong with that.

"Anything else?" She wiped her hands and mouth with a napkin. "Or are you going to concede that you eat like a child?" Her smirk pushed him over the edge.

"I'm not conceding anything."

"Then what do you eat that a kid doesn't? I dare you to find one thing. Just one." She leaned forward.

It was time to win this game. "Pussy."

Her eyes widened and her mouth dropped open.

"I love it. As a matter of fact"—his nostrils flared as her eyes darkened with desire—"it's my favorite dish. Maybe you should serve it to me one day." He leaned forward. "How about tonight?"

"Ah…uhm…You win." She stood and almost ran from the room.

CHAPTER 7: ADRIAN

Adrian was exhausted. He'd spent the last few days working twelve hour shifts to fix computer issues caused by an upgrade. It was resolved now and all he wanted was to shower, eat and sleep.

He stepped into his apartment and stopped. Ellie was bent over the couch folding laundry. His eyes roamed over her ass and his hands itched to touch her. Ever since the fajita night she'd avoided him, spending most of her time hiding in her room. "Hey." He closed the door behind him.

She jumped. "Oh, you scared me. I didn't expect you home so early."

"Well, I am." He undid his tie. She didn't need to sound so unhappy about it.

She tossed the rest of the unfolded laundry back into the basket and walked toward her room.

"Where are you going?" He should be relieved that she was avoiding him because he no longer had to see her walking around the house half-naked, but instead he was pissed. They were roommates. Friends of a sort and if she was upset, she should talk to him, not ignore him.

"I thought you'd want to watch TV."

"I don't. I'm beat. I'll be going to bed which means you don't have to hide in your room." He swung out his arm. "You have free roam of the house."

"I haven't been hiding. I've been reading."

"Bullshit."

"I'm not lying. I don't like to watch TV all the time. Sometimes I like to read."

"Me too but that doesn't mean this isn't bullshit. You've been avoiding me ever since I won our little argument."

"I have not. I've been trying to be a *considerate* roommate."

"What is that supposed to mean?" The way she'd stressed that word had made his temper click up another notch.

"Oh, it can mean so many things. Like maybe noticing when someone cleans the apartment and washes all the laundry."

"Let me pat you on the back for running the vacuum through the place." It did look better but he didn't give a shit. "I do my share of cleaning and you fucking live here too."

"I didn't mean that you didn't clean." She took a deep breath. "I just meant that I'm being considerate by reading in my room."

"You should look up the definition of the word. Both words actually—clean and considerate."

"Excuse me?" She was pissed now.

Good because it was time they released some tension. He'd rather do it by fucking, but since that was off the table a fight would have to suffice.

"I'll show you." He strode into the kitchen, knowing what he'd find before he stepped one foot inside. "A considerate roommate would put the dishes in the dishwasher and so would someone who spent the day *cleaning* the apartment."

"I put them away before I go to bed." She stood in the doorway, frowning at him.

"Why not when you're done using them?" He pushed past her. She'd had no problem putting him in a tidy, little box when she'd been done using him.

"It's one plate and some silverware. What's the big deal?"

"The big deal is you never pick up your shit." He grabbed her shoes from the floor by the couch. "I see you vacuumed around these." He shook his head. "There's a place by the door for shoes, but do you use it? No. All my shoes are there, but your shoes are special. They get to sit in the living room like a fucking pet."

"What's your problem today?" She grabbed her shoes from him and dropped them by the others.

"Nothing." He was horny as fuck that was his problem. "Except you're a slob."

"Me? You aren't a joy to live with either."

"What do I do?" He was a great roommate. Unlike her, he actually was considerate, picking up after himself, keeping the TV volume low, being extra quiet when he left for work and not slapping her ass whenever she walked by. It didn't get more considerate than that. Plus, he never walked around in clothes so tight she could measure his cock, not that she'd notice if he did.

"Oh yeah, you're perfect except let's see…" She tapped her lip with her finger. "Who leaves one swallow of orange juice in the container? Who takes the last cold can of soda from the fridge and doesn't add more? Not me."

"I don't see the reason to finish something if I don't want that last swallow. There's always another carton in there."

"And two cartons take up more space."

"One extra carton doesn't fill the refrigerator."

"One? You do the same thing with milk and the two liters of soda."

"I'm not going to dump it out or drink more than I want."

"Fine."

"Is that all I do that annoys you? If it is, it's still way better than living with you."

"Hardly. You also use all the hot water. I've never known anyone who takes longer to shower than you do." She gave him a snide look. "I seem to remember someone bragging about taking such fast showers he made superheroes jealous. What happened to that guy?"

He almost said that guy now spent the time in the shower making sure his balls didn't turn blue because some woman paraded around the house half-naked. He needed to get away from her before he said something he'd regret or grabbed her, bent her over the couch and fucked her. "Speaking of showers, I think I'll go take one now."

"No. Let me go first so I can have some hot water. I was just getting ready to shower."

"Too bad. You should've done it when you got home, just like I'm going to do." He headed for his room.

"I was cleaning and doing the laundry." Ellie ran after him, grabbing his arm. "Please, let me shower first."

"You're welcome to join me but only if you promise to keep your hands to yourself. Remember the rules." He strode into his room, smiling at the thought of the steam that had to be coming from her ears right now.

CHAPTER 8: ELLIE

Ellie stared after Adrian. As if she'd touch him. The damn man didn't even have the decency to shut his bedroom door.

He pulled off his shirt, displaying all those lean muscles like a treat she wasn't allowed to taste. He turned so his front was completely displayed—six pack abs, light dusting of hair that trailed down his chest and beneath his pants.

"You can look all you want but no touching." He smirked.

She wanted to scream but her mouth was too dry. He pulled off his belt, his hands moving to his button. By the growing bump in his pants, this was affecting him too and she was glad. Lately, all he'd done was frown at her and snap.

He dropped his pants, his cock hard in his black boxers. The drying in her mouth was replaced by drool.

She forced her eyes to his face as she cleared her throat. "Don't use all the hot water. I'm begging you." Her eyes dropped back to his crotch. She hadn't meant to use those exact words but since she had, she was happy to see his dick get even bigger.

"I'm going to stay in the shower until every last drop of hot water is gone." He pushed his underwear down before walking into the bathroom.

She was so glad he didn't turn around because she couldn't pull her eyes away from his tight ass. She didn't even blink until he disappeared into the other room. She took a deep breath, fanning herself as she walked into her bathroom and turned on the water. Damn it. The water line went to his bathroom first. The best she'd get was tepid water. It'd be like showering in a pond. She wasn't bathing in lukewarm water. She wanted hot and she was going to get it.

Do not touch. Well, two could play that game. She pulled off her clothes and walked naked into his room.

CHAPTER 9: ADRIAN

Adrian leaned his hands against the wall of the shower, letting the hot water stream down his back. It'd taken him all of about five strokes to come but he was still frustrated, angry and his balls were backed up. He was going to have calluses on his dick from jerking off so much. He needed Ellie to crawl into his bed but by the look on her face, that was going to happen about as soon as the sun rose in the west.

Okay. He had to think. He missed watching TV with her and talking. They had a lot in common. He worked in cyber security and she was a forensic accountant. There was a lot of crossover between the jobs. They were both close to their families and liked the same kind of books and movies. She was driving him crazy, but he didn't want her to move out and he didn't want her avoiding him.

He was going to have to talk to her about not running around half-naked. He'd still want her but at least he wouldn't be bumping into things with his cock.

The shower door slid open. Ellie stood there naked, her tits lush and large, her nipples pointing right at him and making his cock rise again. His eyes traveled south. Her body was soft, hips round and her pussy neatly shaved with only a small triangle of hair between her legs. Fuck he wanted to drop to his knees and feast or grab her and toss her on the sink and slide into her, fucking her hard and fast until she screamed.

"Move, please. Some of that hot water is for me." She flipped her hand in a "get out of my way" gesture.

He stepped back without thinking. Right now, she could tell him to jump in front of a car and he'd do it as long as she let him stare at her tits. She got into the shower, her back to his front, and tipped her head, sighing as the hot water cascaded over her body. She grabbed the shampoo and began to wash her hair.

His shower was big, but it'd shrunk to the size of a tiny closet. Of course, his cock was taking up more room than it had earlier. "Want me to help?" He had to touch her. He was pretty sure he'd die if he didn't.

"Nope. That'd be touching." She glanced at him over her shoulder a superior expression on her face. "Wouldn't it?"

"Yes, it would." Somehow, he managed to force the words out of his mouth even with his jaw clenched so hard it was about to shatter. So, she hadn't come in here to fuck. She'd come in to torture him but there was no way he was backing down.

He waited while she soaped her hair. She turned, letting the water wash away the shampoo and giving him a perfect view of her tits. He wanted to bend and take those pretty little pink nubs into his mouth, but he didn't move. When her hair was clear of suds, he said, "We're going to have to switch places."

"Why?" She grabbed the soap and a washcloth.

"I need to wash my hair." He stepped closer, deciding that his cock bumping into her only counted as touching if it slid inside her pussy.

"You haven't done that yet?"

"I was busy." He gave her a look that dared her to ask.

"Oh." Her gaze dropped down his body. "Doesn't look like you did a good job."

"What can I say? Nothing can keep a good man down." He reached around her, his arm and chest coming perilously close to her breasts and shoulder but not close enough to touch. He grabbed the shampoo. "If you don't move and I bump into you that's your fault."

"Not if you're the one reaching." She scurried to the side. "Now, you can move."

He did and they switched places. He could swear the heat from her body was even hotter than the water. He squeezed some shampoo into his hands and washed his hair. His dick grew as he watched her staring at his chest like she'd never seen anything like it. He let the water wash away the soap and then grabbed the conditioner.

"Want some?' He held it out.

She leaned around him, hanging the washcloth on the bar and putting the soap on the rack. Her breasts coming so close to his chest that he could almost feel their satiny texture. She straightened and offered him her hand. He

32

squeezed the bottle, the thick, creamy fluid filling her palm. Fuck. He was so turned on right now he was going to explode. He squirted conditioner in his palm, much more quickly than he'd done for her, and rubbed it in his hair.

She mirrored his motions, her hands raising to her scalp. Her mouth opened slightly as her breathing increased, making her tits sway. His own chest heaved like he'd just run from a bear or a witch. Yes, that was more like it. He was trying to escape a witch.

She reached around him again, grabbing the soap. She straightened and it slipped from her fingers. They both stared at it between his feet.

"Are you going to get that?" His voice sounded like he'd eaten gravel and his cock was so hard it was dripping precum.

Her gaze met his, and he could tell by the hard gleam that she'd accepted his challenge. "I am." She bent slowly never taking her eyes from his.

Fuck. In a few seconds she was going to get a facial. She stared up at him as her hand skimmed across the tile for the soap.

"I'm having a hard…time finding it."

He braced his hands on the wall and shower door because otherwise he was going to grab her head and shove his cock down her throat.

"Here it is." She stood and the air came back into his lungs.

She snatched her washcloth from the bar and lathered it with soap before rubbing her neck, down her chest and then across her breasts. His arms shook rattling the shower door.

"Is something wrong?" she asked innocently.

"Ellie…" It was a plea.

"What's the matter? Are you regretting not saving some hot water for me?"

He had two choices. Surrender and fuck her, if she'd let him, or retreat. Her hand with the washcloth slid between her legs. The sound that came from his throat was more animal than human as he burst from the shower, grabbing a towel and stumbling into his room.

CHAPTER 10: ELLIE

Ellie wasn't sure if she was thrilled to see Adrian run or pissed. She did know that she was frustrated beyond words. She stayed in the shower for a few more minutes, letting the hot water do whatever it could to cool her temper and her libido.

She turned off the water and opened the shower door. Adrian had taken the only towel and she's been too bent on teaching him a lesson to remember to grab one. She squeezed as much water from her hair as she could and walked out of the bathroom. She could've found a hand towel or something to cover herself but fuck him. This was all his fault. He was the one driving her crazy—crazy horny. It was only fair he felt it too.

Adrian's bedroom was empty. Damn. She walked into the living room and he was by the door, keys in hand.

"Where are you going?" She loved how his eyes darkened when they trailed across her body, spending a lot of time on her breasts before moving lower. The juncture between her thighs ached for his touch, his cock. She took a step toward him. She hadn't meant to, but her body just moved.

"Ellie…" Her name was a whispered plea just like before in the shower.

"Yes." She moved closer, like he was pulling her with a string.

"Stop."

She took another step.

"If you don't stop"—each word was forced from him like he was prying it from a vise—"I'm going to do more than touch you."

"You made that rule, not me."

His eyes lifted to hers. "Don't fuck with me."

"Why not? You've been fucking with me. Undressing in front of me. Smelling so damn good when we watch TV that I want to scream."

"You've done worse." This time he took a step toward her. "Running around in those short shorts or pants so tight I can see your pussy lips."

"You cannot." If he could, that was embarrassing.

"I can." He took another step. "I'm giving you one last warning. Put some fucking clothes on or get in my bed."

"Those are my only choices?"

"Or tell me to go. To leave. Right now. Because I can't stay here with you and not touch you." He took the final step, his body so close that she could smell his shampoo. It was the same kind that was in her hair and it was like he was already surrounding her, covering her. "Tell me to leave."

"No." She turned and headed for his room. She

stopped in the doorway and looked over her shoulder. "Are you coming because I'm horny enough to start and finish without you."

CHAPTER 11: ADRIAN

For one second Adrian˙stood frozen in place. This had to be a dream, or some new demented torture Ellie had planned for him. His body didn't care. In the next second, he hurled himself through his apartment like a charging elephant. Nothing was going to stop him or slow him down. He flew into his bedroom, half-believing she wouldn't be there. That this was his brain's illusion from lack of blood, but she was really in his room, naked and crawling onto his bed.

"Stop. Right there." He wanted to memorize this for his old age. She was on her hands and knees, her pale, round ass in the air, begging for his hand.

She stopped and looked at him over her shoulder, her wet hair cascading around her neck and her eyes so brown they were almost black.

He wanted to jump on her and shove himself so far inside her that she screamed. If he touched her, he'd do exactly that, and it'd be excellent, perfect, stupendous but only if she was as hot for him as he was for her. "Are you wet?" *Please, please, please make her be dripping for him.*

"See for yourself."

His body lurched forward but he stopped inches from her. "I...Ellie, if I touch you, I'm going to lose it. I can't be gentle or take it slow."

Her gaze locked with his as she ran her hand between her legs. Her mouth opened and he almost came as her tongue skimmed along her lips. She pulled her hand from her pussy and shifted, offering it to him. He grabbed her wrist. Her fingers were slick and glossy with wetness. He took a deep breath, smelling her arousal before sucking her juices from her fingers.

"Wet enough?" Her eyes darkened.

"Not quite." He dropped her hand and walked to the nightstand, pulling out a handful of condoms and tossing all but one on top by the lamp.

"That's a lot of condoms." She laughed.

"It's a start." He dropped the package on the bed and pulled off his shirt while he kicked off his shoes. "But first, this." He had to have more of her. That little sample on her fingers wasn't near enough. He bent, grabbing her ass spreading it wide and burying his face between her cheeks.

CHAPTER 12: ELLIE

Ellie moaned as Adrian's tongue slid along her slit. Damn, he was good at that, really good. Her fingers dug into the covers as his tongue slipped inside her and his thumb teased her clit.

"Oh…yes…oh…Adrian." She shoved her ass back into his face, needing him to keep doing what he was doing. It'd been too long since she'd felt his touch.

"Don't come." He nipped her butt cheek and shoved two fingers inside her, rubbing against her G-spot.

"I can't…please…" It didn't matter what he said. She was too horny, too on edge. Her body tightened around his fingers.

"Do not come." He slapped her ass as he pulled his hand from between her legs.

"Oh…god." That slap made her body spasm and sent her into overdrive. She needed his fingers on her, in her.

"You cannot come." He grabbed her hair, pulling back her head as he leaned over her. "I'm going to bury my cock so deep inside you that you can't breathe without feeling me. You can't think of anything else but how fucking good

I feel inside you. Then, you can come."

"Yes." She wanted that too. "Hurry." She was so close. She'd been beyond frustrated for weeks and today had pushed her into heat. A stray breeze would probably make her orgasm.

"Play with your clit but do not come." He stepped away and her hands went between her legs. She'd do anything he said as long as he gave her his cock. She didn't want to masturbate quietly in her room anymore. She wanted this—sex raw and desperate. She wanted him.

He lifted off the bed. The sound of his zipper undoing was like music. Her fingers danced over her sensitive bud, faster and harder, making her hips begin to thrust.

"Slow down before you come." He swatted her ass, the sharp pain tangled with her pleasure and she moaned, low and loud.

He knelt behind her. His cock, hot and hard, teased her seam. She pushed back against him. She wanted him inside her now. He took the hint, grabbing her hip with one hand while he thrust into her. She gasped as he made her stretch for him, made her body surrender to his.

He grabbed her other hip, his fingers digging into her soft flesh as he pumped in and out of her. She moaned, dropping her head to the bed which made his dick shift inside her.

"Fuck." He grunted, as he fucked her faster and harder.

Her hands dug into the covers as his cock filled her, igniting her blood until there was nothing left but his body and hers and the music of flesh hitting flesh.

CHAPTER 13: ADRIAN

Adrian wasn't going to last long. Ellie felt too good wrapped around his cock with her ass pointing up at him, white and firm. His fingers dug into the soft flesh of her hips as he buried his cock inside her over and over. Her moans interspersed with the slap of his body against hers making a symphony of sex. She was close; he felt it in her trembles and the way she clutched him. He thrust faster and faster. If she didn't come soon, he was going to embarrass himself. He reached around her waist, his fingers searching between her thighs until they found her clit. He rubbed in circles, keeping pace with his dick. Her back arched and her pussy squeezed him, making him groan. Her hips bucked as she came and he rode her wave of pleasure, shoving into her one more time. He shuddered, emptying himself into her. No, not her, the condom.

For the first time in his adult life, he wanted to fuck without a condom. He wanted to fill her with his cum, mark her as his in the most elemental way. He pulled out of her and flopped onto his back. She dropped to the bed, still on her belly. He took off the condom and tossed it into the garbage by his bed.

Their pants filled the air, but she didn't move. Fuck, had he been too rough? She'd definitely orgasmed but was she regretting it now? He sure as fuck wasn't. He rolled to his side and brushed the hair from her face so he could see her. "Everything okay, babe?"

"Don't call me that and yeah." She lifted onto her elbows, her hair a tangle around her face.

"You sure everything is okay?"

"Yeah. I just don't like being called babe or sweetie or honey. I have a name. Use it."

"Sorry. I didn't know it bothered you."

"Well, it does." She sat up.

"Hold on." He sat up too. She wasn't getting away from him now. "I said I was sorry, and I won't do it again."

"I've told you before and you're still doing it." She looked almost like she was going to cry.

"Hey." He grabbed her around the waist pulling her back against him. "I'm sorry. I don't remember you telling me that, but I know now, and I won't do it again. I promise." It was going to be hard because that's how he thought of her in his head—his babe. His.

"Okay." She didn't sound convinced, but she relaxed, snuggling against him.

He loosened his hold since she was no longer trying to fuck and run. He scooted down on the bed, keeping her close. She leaned up and kissed his jaw and then started to wiggle away.

"Where do you think you're going?" His arms

tightened again.

"Nowhere."

"Then stay here."

"I am but I thought you didn't like to snuggle."

"I don't but this isn't snuggling."

"Really? Then what do *you* call this?" She wrapped her arm around his waist and rested her face against his chest.

"This is making sure you don't sneak away"—he tapped the nightstand with his elbow—"before we use the allotted number of condoms." Now wasn't the time to talk to her about riding bareback.

"Wow. You sure think highly of your stamina."

"I've been storing up."

"I thought you were taking care of that in the shower."

"I was but that doesn't count. That was only for you."

"For me?" She laughed. "You masturbated for me?"

"Yep. For your safety." He tried to keep his tone serious.

"Oh, this I have to hear."

"Okay, but I want you to remember how I'm always looking out for you."

"I will." She laughed again. "I promise."

"Well, I masturbated so I didn't accidentally impale you every time you walked by me."

"You mean like you just did."

"That wasn't an accident. You begged me to impale you."

"Begged? I merely suggested. You were the one begging."

"That's true." He had no problem admitting that since she was naked in his bed. "The good thing is I can go back to quick showers and you can have all the hot water you need."

"As long as you make sure you get all the important places clean in those quick showers of yours."

"You're welcome to inspect my work anytime or even supervise."

"I may have to do just that."

CHAPTER 14: ELLIE

By the time Ellie woke, Adrian was gone. She rolled out of his bed and walked to her bathroom. She wanted to bang her head against the mirror. Last night had been beyond fabulous but it was a huge mistake. She couldn't keep jumping from one relationship to the next.

She grabbed her phone. "Alison, can you meet me for lunch? I need to talk."

"Sure. Is everything okay?"

"Yeah. No. I don't know."

"Oh my god, you slept with him again. Yes!" She sounded like she was going to high-five someone.

"That's not a good thing."

"Oh, but it is. I won the bet with Harker."

"You bet against me? You're supposed to be my friend."

"I am your friend. I took the later date. Harker thought you'd be sleeping together before one week was up at the latest. I said before a month. See. I had your back."

"Yeah, you're great."

"Gotta go. Harker's coming. I can't wait to tell him he

lost. See you at the diner at eleven thirty." Alison hung up.

"Yeah. Sure." What was the point? Her friend was obviously not on her side about this.

She walked into the kitchen. A note sat on the counter.

Sorry I had to leave so early. I made you a PB&J.

"Oh, no." She opened the fridge and pulled out a sandwich container. The damn man had even sliced it into two triangles, exactly how she liked it.

She picked up the sandwich and dropped onto a chair at the table. She liked Adrian a lot and she wanted to be with him, but she didn't want to screw it up by moving this fast. She'd only known him a little over a month. She needed to slow things down between them but that wouldn't happen while she was living here.

Once she moved, they could both take a step back and make sure that this is what they both wanted, but for right now, there was no real way to get that distance. Her body warmed at the thought of sleeping with him every night. She took a bite of the sandwich. PB&J was better than she'd remembered.

CHAPTER 15: ELLIE

Ellie changed her shirt again. She was being stupid. They were just meeting his friends and Alison at Murphy's, but she wanted to look hot. That bartender was way too friendly with Adrian.

The last week had been great. They'd spent the evenings watching TV or talking and later, they'd had sex—wonderful, fabulous sex. Sometimes they had it before dinner too, but they always ended the evening with sex. Her favorite place in the house was their bed. No, it was his bed, not their bed.

She still had to find an apartment. She couldn't move in with him on a permanent basis, at least not yet. Perhaps in a year or so they could take this step, but she really wanted this relationship to last and that meant not rushing everything. She pulled on another shirt. This one had a square neckline that accentuated her breasts. That should keep his eyes on her.

She walked out of her bedroom. Adrian was on the couch watching TV.

"I'm ready." She smiled. "I know. Finally." It'd taken

her longer than it should've, and men didn't like to wait.

"Great. Let's go." He glanced at her and stood, barely noticing her shirt.

Her heart fell to her stomach. Disinterest was the first sign of the end. Damn her. She'd known this would happen and yet she'd let herself believe that maybe he was different.

He frowned at her.

"Look, I'm sorry I took so long." She wanted to slap herself. She had no reason to apologize because he was angry.

"It's fine." He walked to the door and grabbed his keys. He hesitated.

"Are we going or not." She couldn't wait for this night to be done.

He cupped her face and kissed her softly. "Sorry if I seemed pissed. I'm not."

"Please. You have that air of disgusted male who's been made to wait forever."

"Don't do that."

"Do what?" She'd been joking, kind of.

"Act like everything I do and say is just like all the other men you've dated."

"That's not...I'm sorry but guys always get pissed about waiting just like women are bitchy around their periods. Facts are facts." She smiled again but his frown deepened. "I didn't mean anything." She stood on her tiptoes and kissed him.

"For the record"—he rested his hands on her hips,

keeping her close—"I wasn't angry."

"Then why were you frowning at me?"

"I wasn't frowning at you. I was thinking about asking you something."

Her heart stalled. A heart attack would be great right now because if he asked her to move in with him officially...

His hand slipped into his pocket.

Oh God, was he going to propose? He wouldn't do that would he? They barely knew each other. Her heart raced. She should say no, but...

"You know that toy we got for Christmas?"

"What?" She had no idea what he was talking about.

"This." He pulled the vibrator that they'd gotten from Desiree from his pocket. "I was thinking we should try this tonight." His lips quirked up in a sexy smile. "It'll be fun and when we get home...it'll be amazing."

"You're asking me to have a vibrator inside me that you control with your phone while we're out with your friends at a bar. A very crowded, public bar." She'd been preparing for I love you or will you marry me, or even will you move in with me permanently but instead she'd gotten how about I slide a sex toy inside you and show you off to my friends.

"I was." His grin faded fast.

"I don't think so." She pulled away from him.

"Why?"

"Because I don't want to."

"But why?"

"Because I'm not going to sit at the bar and orgasm for your friends."

"I wouldn't do that."

"Then why use it? That's exactly what it's for."

"No. The toy is about trust."

"Please." She flicked the vibrator. "That's about sex, not trust."

"Okay. You know everything." He tossed the toy on the couch and opened the door.

She stepped into the hallway and started down the stairs for what would surely be a long and shitty night.

CHAPTER 16: ADRIAN

By the time they got home, Adrian was more than a little annoyed. It hadn't seemed possible, but the evening had gone downhill from their earlier argument.

Ellie had spent the night laughing and joking with Alison and his friends, but he'd needed a parka to even sit by her with the chilly air she sent his way.

He opened the door to their apartment and stepped aside, letting her enter first. She, of course, headed straight to her bedroom. They'd been sleeping together for almost two weeks, but she still changed in the guest room. He stripped as he headed for their room, tossing his clothes into the laundry basket on the way. He dropped onto the bed and waited…and waited. Oh, hell no. He wasn't going to let her avoid him just because she was mad. He jumped out of bed and stormed out of his room, slamming into her.

"Hey," she squeaked.

"Sorry." He grabbed her shoulders to keep her from falling.

"What's wrong?"

"I thought you were thinking about staying in the guest

room."

She pulled free. "I had considered staying in *my* room."

"Don't push me any more tonight, Ellie." He was about ready to throw her over his shoulder and toss her into his bed.

"Anymore? I didn't do anything."

"You barely spoke to me."

"We talked as much as we needed to."

"You moved away every time I touched you."

She shrugged. "I didn't feel like having you touch me."

"Why? Because I wanted you to trust me enough to try something kinky?"

"No, because you got mad when I wouldn't. I don't have to want to do everything you want to do."

"I wasn't mad because you didn't want to do it. I was pissed because you don't trust me."

"Like you'd wear a shocker on your nuts and give me control."

"You're right, I wouldn't. Not right now because you aren't even part of this relationship."

"Excuse me."

"You haven't moved any of your stuff, not even your toothbrush, into our room. You dress in that other room." He refused to call it her room. "You shower in the other bathroom. Your makeup and clothes are still across the house. The only thing you do in here is fuck me."

"Don't worry. That stops tonight." She turned but his arm wrapped around her waist, stopping her from walking away. "Let me go." She shoved at his hand.

"Stop fighting me and listen." He gripped her arms and spun her around. "If this is more than just fucking to you, then do not go to your room tonight. You can be mad at me. Hell, you don't even have to touch me but if this means something to you then you'll sleep with me tonight. No sex. Just two people who are pissed off at each other but still want to be together." He dropped his hands and took a step back, waiting.

She glared at him before turning and walking to her room.

He stared at the closed door for a long time. He was numb to everything and that was good because when he was able to feel again, it was going to hurt—bad. It was over. They were done. He couldn't force her to feel something for him. He'd been sure that she had. He would've bet money on it, and he would've lost.

Her door opened and she stepped into the living room, stopping when she saw him. She had tears in her big, brown eyes and she didn't say a word as she walked past, giving him a wide berth. She crawled into their bed and rolled to her side away from him.

He turned off the light and got into bed. He wasn't getting laid tonight, but he'd never been happier.

CHAPTER 17: ADRIAN

Adrian checked everything one more time. The table was covered in a dark, red tablecloth that looked perfect with the white dishes. He had a bottle of red wine on the kitchen counter and a bottle of white chilling in the fridge. He also had a six pack of beer because he'd never seen Ellie drink wine, but bottles of beer on the table didn't set the right ambiance for Valentine's Day.

He'd light the candles right after he got back from picking up the dessert from the coffee shop. His sister had sworn that it was the best chocolate cake in town. He grabbed the Valentine's gift and placed it in the center of the table next to the flowers. He'd gone with six roses and a dozen daisies. She'd told him that daisies used to grow wild near her great grandmother's house. She and her sister would spend hours braiding them into strands or playing he-loves-me, he-loves-me-not.

He stared at the gift. He should get her something else. He didn't want to seem cheap. He could swing into the jewelry store on the way home from the coffee shop and buy her a necklace or something.

The alarm on his phone beeped. Shit. It was almost six. He should've left work earlier, but he hadn't expected the lines at the grocery store and florist to be so long. He should've, but he hadn't had a serious girlfriend in a long time. He'd spent most of the last ten years in the desert being shot at.

He turned off the oven and opened it. He'd made enchiladas from scratch. He pulled off the aluminum foil before closing the oven door. By the time he came back from the coffee shop the cheese should be golden brown.

He grabbed his keys and headed out the door. Tonight, was going to be perfect. He'd wine her and dine her and then ask her to move in with him—officially.

They hadn't spoken about their fight the other evening, but every night Ellie was in their bed. She still hadn't moved anything into his room but hopefully, he could convince her to change that tonight. He wanted her makeup cluttering his bathroom and her clothes mixed with his in the closet. This was moving fast, and it terrified him, but he liked her a lot. He might even more than like her.

He entered the coffee shop and stopped. Paige waved at him, making a "sorry" face. Ellie stood at the counter talking to his sister. He walked over to them.

"Hey, Adrian," said Paige. "What brings you here?"

"Hi." Ellie smiled up at him. She looked tired. She should take a nice, relaxing bath. He should insist. They could always reheat dinner. Enchiladas tasted better reheated; he was sure of it.

"Hello." He bent and kissed her.

"I was stopping to pick up some dessert for Valentine's Day," she said.

"Great minds think alike." His arm went around her. If she were near, he had to touch her. "Is it ready, Paige?"

"Yep," said his sister. "Give me one second." She disappeared into the back.

"That's why she wouldn't sell me the cupcakes. I thought she was just the worst salesperson ever." Ellie leaned against him, resting her head on his chest.

"Long day at work?"

"Yeah." She sighed. "I know it's Valentine's Day but all I want to do is curl up on the couch." She looked up at him. "Is that okay with you?"

"Absolutely. I want to stay home with you too." He kissed her again. He really couldn't help it when she looked at him with her eyes soft and her lips parted. "Dinner is almost ready but maybe you should relax in the tub first." He kissed her ear, whispering, "If you ask me nicely, I might even wash your back."

CHAPTER 18: ELLIE

"A bath sounds wonderful." Against her better judgement Ellie was falling for Adrian. She needed to slow things down, just a bit, but she wasn't sure how Adrian would take the news.

A woman had contacted her today about an apartment. She'd called about the place right after she'd moved out of her place. It was close to her work, in a nice area and not too expensive. It'd be perfect except she liked living with Adrian.

"Here you go." Paige came back with a large cake box and put it on the counter.

"What kind is it?" She started to open the package but stopped. "May I?"

"Of course." Adrian handed his sister his card.

"Oh, chocolate." She ran her finger through the frosting and offered it to Adrian.

He wrapped his lips around her finger, sucking and twirling his tongue exactly how she loved it when he did it between her legs. She was pretty sure her face heated by his sexy smirk.

"Good?" she asked.

"You tell me." His grin was downright wicked this time as he reached for the cake.

"I don't think that's a good idea." She grabbed his wrist, her eyes dropping to his crotch. "This is a family place." She slid her finger through the frosting again and slowly licked the chocolate before putting her finger inside her mouth and sucking. "It's delicious but a little cream would make it perfect."

"That can be arranged." His eyes darkened to that forest at midnight color that told her body sex was coming—great, wild sex.

"I ordered the vanilla cream with chocolate frosting for Mom's birthday next week." Paige stared at the computer, oblivious to the underlying conversation. "You can try that one then."

"Your mother's birthday?"

"I told you about it last week," he said as he took his card back from his sister.

"Oh. Yeah. That's right." She'd hoped he'd reconsider taking her. They'd only been together a few weeks. It was way too early to meet the parents.

"You are going to be there, right?" asked Paige. "Mom and Dad can't wait to meet you and ignore my sisters, especially the older ones. They're quite protective of Adrian."

"Oh….uhm…I'm sorry but I can't make it." She felt like a heel.

"Oh." Paige's face fell.

"You can't? Why not?" Adrian stared down at her. The hot, dark look in his eyes was gone.

She glanced at his sister. "Let's talk about this at the apartment." She took his hand and smiled at Paige. "Thanks, and happy Valentine's Day." Hopefully, someone was going to have one because unless she could perform some magic her quiet night was probably going to turn into a fight.

CHAPTER 19: ADRIAN

Adrian waited in the parking lot for Ellie to get out of her car before heading up the stairs. He was trying really hard to keep his temper in check.

"I'm so tired. I think I'll run the bath right away, if that's okay with you?"

"It's not." He'd told her about his mother's party and he damn well expected her to go. He opened the door and she proceeded him inside.

"Oh, it smells delicious." She stopped, looking into the kitchen. "It looks lovely. You shouldn't have gone to all this trouble." She kissed him but he didn't kiss her back.

"It's our first Valentine's together. Why shouldn't I go to the trouble?" He dropped the cake box on the table.

"Oh...I didn't mean...It's sweet. That's all."

"Do you think it's our first Valentine's Day together as a couple or is this just a Valentine's Day with a guy you're fucking?"

"Please don't make a big deal out of this."

"Out of what? There are so many things. Like how you never call this our apartment or even your apartment."

"Because it's not. You invited me to stay until I found a place." She paused and then added. "Ms. Mapeltrix texted me today about an apartment that just opened up. She said I could come by and see it tomorrow."

"You're still looking?" He had no idea how to process this. He'd been planning on moving forward as a couple and she'd been planning on moving out.

"Ah…not exactly. She contacted me."

"Did you tell her you'd be by to see it tomorrow?"

"Ah…I was going to tell you—"

"It's a simple fucking question, Ellie. Did you tell her that you'd look at the apartment?"

"Yeah. I didn't know how you felt. I've already been here a lot longer than I'd…than either of us had planned. I didn't want to impose any longer."

"Impose? Is that what this is to you? An imposition?"

"No. Of course not." She touched his arm. "Adrian, I like you but…this thing between us is moving too fast. I don't want to do that again." Her hand entwined with his. "I don't want this to end but I think we should slow down a bit. We should make sure that we both want this, and it isn't just feelings we have because we're living together." She kissed him. "Please don't be angry."

"We can slow it down without you moving out." His hands moved to her hips. He didn't want her to leave.

"I don't think we can." She wrapped her arms around his waist, resting her head on his chest. "I've done this too many times, rebounding from one relationship to the next and every time it ends badly."

"All relationships end badly until you find the right one." He kissed the top of her head. "Everyone goes through that."

She laughed. "Yeah, but I'm the idiot who keeps making the same mistake over and over again."

CHAPTER 20: ELLIE

Ellie knew she'd screwed up the second the words were out of her mouth. If she hadn't, the stiffening of Adrian's body would've made it clear. It was like hugging a statue. She swore she could even feel the cold emanating from him. "I didn't mean that like it sounded."

"Really? Then how you did mean it because obviously I'm an idiot too." He untangled her arms from around him.

"I know you're not like Marc."

"I don't think you do."

"I do, Adrian. You're nothing like Marc and I know that." She had to make him understand that taking it slow had nothing to do with him. "But we've only known each other a little over six weeks and we're already living together. That's fast by anyone's standards. We need to slow this down."

"You told me you dated a couple of other guys before we hooked up again. If you were living with one of them, would you be insisting that the two of you take it slow?"

"I wouldn't be living with one of them."

"Why is that?"

"Because they wouldn't move in with someone they just met."

"You're not talking about those specific guys, are you?"

"What? Yeah. Of course."

"I thought the little liar was gone but here she is again."

"Fine. No, I wasn't talking about either of them specifically, but no one moves in with someone this quickly. It's crazy."

"No one except guys like me."

"I didn't say that." This was spiraling out of control.

"You didn't have to. I'm stupid but not that stupid." He headed for the door.

"Where are you going?" Her stomach churned like she was going to puke.

"Someplace where guys like me hang out. You keep treating me like your exes I may as well act like them." He slammed the door behind him.

Ellie stood there for a long time, her heart wanting to call him back but her mind telling her that she wasn't wrong. They were moving too fast. She walked into the kitchen. The table looked perfect—a romantic dinner for two. She'd ruined tonight but she wouldn't be pushed into moving too fast. Not again. He could blow off some steam and then they could talk rationally when he came back.

CHAPTER 21: ELLIE

Ellie trudged up the stairs to the apartment. Today had been horrible. Adrian hadn't come home last night, and he hadn't even bothered to answer her texts or voice mails. He could be hurt or dead. *He's in bed with some other woman just like all the others.* She didn't want to believe it, but she couldn't help it.

On top of that, she'd wasted the entire morning going to see that apartment. She opened the door and stopped on the threshold. Adrian sat on the couch watching TV. Relief surged through her. He wasn't dead or hurt...which left..."You could've at least answered my texts to let me know you were okay." She closed the door behind her and walked toward her room.

"Why? Did your other boyfriends do that? I'm new at treating women like shit. You're going to have to give me some pointers."

"You don't need pointers. You're doing a fantastic job." She threw her purse on the bed. "The cheating is the big thing, and it seems you got that down pat."

"So now I fucked someone because I didn't answer

your texts?"

"Didn't you?" She crossed her arms over her chest. It was time for his performance. He'd lie and flirt, telling her how he'd never do something like that.

"I'm not answering that."

"Wow. You jumped ahead. That should be your second line. I can't wait until next time when it's all my fault." Her voice cracked. She'd been such a fool. "Am I suddenly cold? Does your dick freeze when it's inside me?"

"I didn't sleep with anyone." He stood. "I don't fucking cheat but you can't see that because all you see when you look at me is Marc and the other assholes you dated."

"I'm supposed to just believe you." She had no idea where these men learned their audacity, but they should teach a course.

"Yes. That's what a relationship is. Without trust there isn't one, but I guess that's what you've been telling me since the beginning. I just didn't want to listen. Instead, I tried to show you who I am. Show you that you could trust me with everything, but I'm done. I can't do this anymore."

Her heart stopped and the air in the house seem to evaporate. He walked into his room and she followed, trying to think of something to say to fix this. He grabbed a duffel bag from the closet and started throwing clothes into it.

"What are you doing?

"I can't stay here with you." He stuffed some more Tshirts into the bag and walked back to the closet. "Text me when you move into your apartment."

"Oh."

He glanced at her. "You did get it, didn't you?"

"Uhm…yeah."

"You're lying again aren't you?" He studied her closely.

"No. Yes. It didn't work out. She rented it right before I got there, but it doesn't matter. I'll go. You don't have to leave."

He grabbed his bag. "I'll go back to Mitch's. He said I could stay in his spare room. Text me when you find a place." He stopped in front of her. "I hope you find somewhere that makes you happy." He walked past her and left the apartment.

Ellie's legs gave out and she slid down the wall. Her chest so tight and twisted she half-feared she was having a heart attack. She curled onto the floor and cried, great, big sobs. It was over and…it hurt so badly. She hadn't expected that. She's spent years with Marc and hadn't felt anything but anger and relief when it'd ended.

But this time, it felt like he'd torn out her heart and had taken it with him. She sat up, wiping her eyes. This was for the best. They'd been moving too fast. It would've ended just like her other relationships eventually. She walked to her bedroom and grabbed her phone from her purse. "Alison, Adrian left me." She tried but couldn't stop the sob from slipping past her lips.

"I'll be right over. Where are you?" asked Alison.

68

"At his place."

"But you said that you broke—"

"We did and he left." She sobbed harder. He was the nicest guy she'd ever met, and she'd treated him like he was an asshole.

CHAPTER 22: ELLIE

A knock on the door made Ellie pull the pillow over her face. Her head pounded and her throat was dry like she'd slept with a rag in her mouth.

"I got it," Alison mumbled from the living room. Her friend had come over for lunch and the two of them had drank through dinner.

"Mrs. White. Hey. Come in," said Alison.

Ellie sat up in bed. What was her mother doing here? She stumbled out of the bedroom, stopping in the doorway.

"Ellie, your Mom's here." Alison grabbed her pillow from the couch. "I'm going to sleep while you two talk."

"Mom? What are you doing here?"

"Alison texted me last night."

"Alison?" She wanted to strangle her friend.

"Seemed like a good idea at the time. You wouldn't listen to me." Alison squeezed past her into the bedroom. "I need sleep." She shoved Ellie into the living room and closed the door.

"Mom, I'm sorry about this. I didn't know she texted you."

"Ellie." Her mom opened her arms.

For one second Ellie just stood there and then everything imploded. Adrian had left. It was really over, and it hurt so bad she could barely think straight. She ran across the room and her mom's arms wrapped around her, holding her tight. She buried her face in her mother's shoulder, fighting back the tears. If she started, she wouldn't stop.

"You smell like booze." Mom kissed the top of her head. "Go take a shower and I'll make something for you to eat."

She dropped her arms and stepped back, making a face. "I'm really not hungry." She'd puke if she ate anything.

"It'll be bland. I promise. Now, go. I have to meet your dad later."

Ellie came out of the bathroom, feeling somewhat human again after the shower. Her mother sat at the table, scrolling through her phone and sipping a cup of tea. In front of the chair next to her sat a plate with eggs and toast, a bottle of water and another cup of tea.

"I'll never understand your dislike of coffee. You should definitely try it after a night of drinking." Mom put the teacup down.

"I don't plan on having any more nights like this." The way she felt right now, she'd never drink again. She dropped onto the chair and picked up the toast, taking a small bite. It was lightly buttered, and it didn't make her want to vomit, so that was a plus.

"Alison said something about this guy leaving. The text didn't make too much sense, but I got the feeling she wasn't talking about Marc."

"No. Adrian." She tore at the toast.

"The young man who drove you home for Christmas?"

"Yes." She tossed the tiny piece of bread she'd been playing with into her mouth.

"He's a good-looking man." Mom smiled and then stopped. "Not that looks are what's important." Her lips lifted a little. "But it doesn't hurt."

"Not when they're that good looking." She took another bite of toast.

"Too attractive? That's not possible. Unless…was he arrogant?"

"Yeah, but not in a bad way. He was funny about it. Cocky and cute and so nice." She wiped at her eyes. "But it's over."

"I'm sorry. What happened?" Mom took a sip of her tea.

"We had a fight on Valentine's Day, and he left. He didn't come home until the next day."

"And?"

"And he cheated on me." She'd thought that was obvious.

"Oh, that's what Alison meant by…" Mom shook her head. "Never mind. Her text needed a bit of deciphering. It was late when she texted and by the look of both of you this morning, she must've been a bit wasted."

"Sorry. She shouldn't have bothered you."

"It's no bother. You should've told me that you found someone else. Last I heard you'd broken up with Marc."

"I didn't say anything because I wasn't really with Adrian."

"This is his place, right?"

"Ah…how did you—"

"This isn't your apartment and I know Alison is staying with her mother. None of this is your furniture. It looks like a single guy's place—large TV, comfortable couch, nothing on the walls, no knickknacks—but you weren't sleeping in the master bedroom. So, you two were living together but not as a couple."

"Not exactly." Her face heated. Her parents knew she'd lived with Marc but talking about this with her mom was a little embarrassing. "We were kind of a couple."

"Hmm. Did he know you were only *kind of* a couple?" Mom's eyes darted to the counter. "Did you buy the cake for yourself for Valentine's Day?"

"No." The cake was in a pretty pink box with hearts on it and tiny cupids. It had obviously been for Valentine's Day.

"Is this what you got him for Valentine's Day?" Mom held up the gift from Adrian which Ellie hadn't opened. It didn't seem right since they weren't together anymore.

"No. That was from him."

"Looks to me like he thought you were more than *kind of* a couple." Mom put the gift down next to her cup. "He seemed like a very nice man, but you have to decide if he's right for you."

"He isn't."

"Then why are you so upset?" Mom took a sip of her tea, watching Ellie closely.

"Because he's perfect and I...I..." She started crying. "When he cheats, he's going to destroy me."

"Oh, honey." Mom leaned over, wrapping her arm around Ellie.

"I love him, Mom. I really love him but I...can't feel like this. I'll never survive when he cheats on me. I won't." She sobbed harder. "I thought I loved Marc, but I didn't, not like this. I'd just settled for him. I thought he'd make a good father and that we wanted the same things but with Adrian....I can't stop thinking about him. We talked all the time. He's my best friend and I miss him. It hurts so bad."

Mom squeezed her tight and kissed the top of her head. "I know, honey." She leaned away, wiping Ellie's cheeks. "Let me tell you about when your father and I separated."

She sat back, taking a sip of her tea and another bite of her toast. Mom and Dad never told any of them about that time.

"I was sure your father was cheating on me."

"Dad?" Her father would never...

"Yes." Mom's eyes grew sad. "I was so hurt. Devastated. That's when I kicked him out. He tried to talk to me, to explain but I wouldn't listen. I was so sure I was right. I had evidence."

"What kind of evidence?" She'd had that picture of

Marc and that woman but before that she'd had her suspicions just like she did now with Adrian.

Mom hesitated. "It was something like a receipt."

"A receipt? To a hotel or…Wait. What's like a receipt?" Her mother wasn't usually this secretive.

"Stop asking so many questions. Let's just say that I had paper evidence but instead of talking to him about it, I assumed things. Then when I saw his car somewhere it shouldn't be…I thought I knew for sure but—"

"Did he cheat on you?" If her father had cheated, then there was no hope for her or anyone. Dad adored Mom. "How did you get past that? How did you forgive him?" Some couples did but she didn't think she'd be able to.

"No, he didn't cheat. I was wrong. I almost ruined the best thing in my life…besides you children, of course…over nothing but doubt and suspicion."

"This is different."

"Is it? How do you know he cheated? Did you ask him?"

"He denied it, but they always do," she said.

"They?"

"Yeah…guys. You know. Like him."

"Guys like him. What exactly does that mean?" asked Mom.

"You saw him. He's the same kind of guy I always fall for. Athletic. Attractive. Alpha male. Caveman."

Mom laughed. "I don't know about the caveman part, but he is definitely athletic, attractive and alpha. Why is that bad?"

75

"Because they all cheat. It's in their nature. They're attractive. Women throw themselves at them and they never refuse."

"So, you think all attractive men are like this?"

"Maybe not all but everyone that I've known." And every guy she'd dated.

"You know our neighbors, Mr. and Mrs. Simms."

"Yeah." Sometimes talking to her mom was like traveling through a maze.

"Do you think he's attractive?"

"Him? No." The man had a comb-over, a beer belly, and bad breath.

"He's cheating on his wife."

"How do you know and who would want a guy like him?"

"Your father and I saw him with a woman who wasn't his wife when we went to dinner one night."

"Maybe she was a sister or a friend."

"I certainly hope not. They were making out at the table. Okay, they weren't making out, but they were definitely kissing with tongue."

"Eww. Why did you tell me this? I'm never going to be able to say hi to him again."

"Because he's not good looking and he cheats." Mom stood and gave her another hug. "Honey, everyone can cheat, both men and women, but not everyone will. You have to open your heart and take a chance. Get to know the man. Trust your gut and your instincts, not your past." She kissed Ellie's cheek. "Talk to him. If you truly think Adrian is the type of man to lie and cheat, then walk away and never look back, but if you're judging him solely on your past that's not fair to either of you."

"How do I know for sure? I don't want to be hurt again."

"You never know for sure and the only way to never be hurt is to stop living. You should think about why you feel this strongly about Adrian after less than two months, when you didn't feel that way about Marc after almost three years." Mom touched her cheek. "Trust your instincts and your heart."

CHAPTER 23: ADRIAN

"Hey, you got a visitor." Mitch leaned in the doorway to Adrian's office.

"Who?" He had no idea who'd come to his office. This was a firm for private investigators, and he worked in cyber security. His family wouldn't even text or call unless it was an emergency.

"I'm going to let you guess. It's a woman. You don't want to talk to her."

"Shit." He wasn't ready to see Ellie yet. He didn't know if he'd ever be.

"It gets better. She bumped into Annie."

"I can't believe I'm going to say this but please tell me it's one of my sisters." He couldn't think of anyone worse for Ellie to have met than Annie, the girlfriend of his CEO.

Annie was great—friendly, funny, a great cook and cute. She was also the biggest busybody he'd ever met and that was saying something because he'd grown up around six sisters and their friends. Annie didn't seem to be able to stop herself from getting involved in the love lives of the employees. Most of them adored her for it but he didn't need any help. What he needed was to get over Ellie and the only way to do that was to avoid her.

"It's not your sister. It's your stalker."

"Don't call her that." He grabbed his gym bag from the floor.

"What should I call her? She's been texting and calling you." Mitch followed him down the hallway.

"She wants to talk. I don't. It's nothing more than that."

"And now she shows up at your workplace. If she were a man and you were a woman, what would you say about this?"

"Shut up. Okay?"

"Suit yourself but when you end up tied to a bed…" Mitch's face scrunched up. "Let me clarify. I mean tied to a bed without consent." He grinned. "With consent I'm sure it's awesome but without…not so much."

"Where is she?" He didn't want to see her, but he also didn't want to listen to his friend. It was bringing back too many memories and he couldn't see Ellie with his dick standing tall and waving hello.

"If you're talking about Ellie"—Annie stepped from Patrick's office—"she's in here. She said you won't answer her texts or phone calls." She frowned at him. "Adrian, I thought you were a good guy."

"Stay here and help me out," he whispered to Mitch.

"You're on your own." His so-called friend slapped him on his back. "As always, Annie, nice to see you." He waved at Patrick who sat at his desk in his office a half-smile on his face.

"Coward," Adrian whispered.

"In this case, yep. See you at the Club tonight?" asked Mitch.

Adrian's eyes met Ellie's. She looked worried and tired, like she hadn't been getting much sleep. Well, neither had he. "Yeah. I'll be there after I work out." He stepped into the office.

Patrick stood. "Adrian, Ellie would like to speak with you." He held out his hand. "Annie, I think this is our cue to leave."

"Leave?" Annie took Patrick's hand. "Not yet." She turned to Adrian. "You'd better stop ignoring her. If you don't want to see her that's fine"—she sent a soft smile toward Ellie before continuing—"but don't ignore her." She dropped Patrick's hand and walked over to Adrian. "It's not nice." She gave him a hug and whispered, "Listen to what she has to say. You're not happy. She's not happy. Maybe if you talk to her you can both be happy." She stepped back and held out her hand. "Patrick, I'm ready now."

"Faster than I'd thought."

She made a face at him.

He turned to Adrian. "Do what Annie says."

"Is that an order from my boss?" He didn't need anyone in his business.

"No. That'd be unethical." Patrick smiled but it wasn't friendly. "However, part of your job description is to work wherever your boss needs you. I believe we have some vacancies in the kitchen with my contractor." He pulled Annie close.

"You wouldn't really do that, would you?" He didn't even want to think about eight hours of Annie lecturing him about his love life.

"Hey, I don't like that you're using working with me as a punishment," said Annie.

"Don't think of it as a punishment," said Patrick. "Think of it as a man being given the opportunity listen to your advice. Kind of like a motivational speaker."

"That is better." Annie grinned at Patrick. "But I doubt he'll think so."

"Sounds exactly like a punishment to me," Adrian muttered.

"I'm going to pretend I didn't hear that." Annie tugged on Patrick's hand. "Let's go home."

They left, closing the door behind them.

He glanced at Ellie and then looked away. It hurt too much to see her. "Did you find an apartment? I told you to text me when you did."

"You don't answer my texts."

"I promise, I'll answer that one."

"Adrian, I'm sorry. Can we please talk about this?"

"There's nothing to talk about but go ahead. Talk. I don't want you coming back here, and I definitely don't want to be assigned kitchen duty."

"Your boss wouldn't really do that, would he?"

Adrian shrugged. "I don't know."

"I won't come back. I promise."

"You shouldn't have come here this time."

"I'm sorry but I didn't know what else to do. You won't answer my texts or my phone calls."

"Because I don't want to talk to you." He swallowed. Fuck this hurt. "I can't, Ellie. I can't be around you right now."

"Adrian, please come home. Let's work this out."

His eyes met hers at her use of the word home. "I'll think about it."

"Thank you." She moved toward him.

"Don't." He held up his hand.

She stopped. "Okay. Sure."

He hated that hurt in her eyes and this time he'd put it there. "I'll be home after I work out. We can talk then."

"I thought you worked out in the morning."

There it was, that tone filled with suspicion. "Forget it. You haven't changed. You still don't trust me."

"What? I never said—"

"What do you think I've been doing since I left? And don't fucking lie to me. I want the truth."

Her eyes widened before dropping to her hands. "It doesn't matter what you've been doing because we're broken up."

"Have you fucked anyone?"

Her eyes snapped to his. "Of course not. I…I want to be with you."

"But you think I'm out there fucking different women every night."

"I'm not the one going to the sex club with my friend.

I've been there; I know what goes on."

"I'm sorry, Ellie. I can't be with someone who doesn't trust me." His heart was gone, annihilated. He wasn't sure there was even a small piece left to heal. "All I've ever wanted was to make you smile. To make you happy. On Christmas Eve you looked so sad but then you were talking to someone on the phone and your smile…" He touched his heart. "I wanted that. I wanted to give you that, but I can't. I can't make you smile when you don't trust me, and I can't force you to trust me." He took one long look at her, trying to memorize everything even the hurt he'd given her. "Goodbye, Ellie." He turned and walked away trying to ignore her soft sob that burned his soul.

CHAPTER 24: ELLIE

Ellie moved through the next few days like she was in a fog. She got up, went to work and came home but it wasn't home because Adrian wasn't here. Every night she told herself she'd look for an apartment but instead she curled on the couch, hugging his pillow. She had to pull herself together and she'd start this weekend. Tomorrow was Saturday. She'd go to the gym or for a long walk, anything to get herself moving, and tonight she'd cook.

She grabbed the mail on the way up the stairs to the apartment. She'd change and then go grocery shopping. She could swing by Mitch's place and give Adrian his mail except he didn't want to see her anymore. It was like someone had punched her in the stomach. Adrian was the best guy in the world, and she'd lost him. No, she'd chased him away.

She opened the door and stepped into the apartment. She didn't have the energy to cook, let alone go shopping. She'd eat leftover pizza and cry herself to sleep, just like last night. She dropped onto the couch and flipped through the mail, putting Adrian's to the side. The rest was junk mail—flyers for local takeout, a letter for new insurance…and a letter addressed to her. She didn't recognize the return address. She opened it, scanning the note inside.

"You've got to be kidding me." She read it again. It was from La Petite Mort Club. The application Marc had pestered her into filling out had been denied due to conflict of interest with another member.

"No. No way." Her exhaustion from earlier disappeared. She was furious with Adrian. "If he wants to fuck a different woman every night at La Petite Mort Club, I don't care, but damn it, he's not going to stop me from doing the same…with a guy." She headed for the door but stopped halfway there. She wasn't going to that club dressed in her work clothes.

Adrian and Ethan St. Johns were going to get a piece of her mind. She didn't want to be a member of the Club, but she wasn't going to let them exclude her just because Adrian couldn't stand to be around her anymore.

CHAPTER 25: ADRIAN

Adrian sat at the bar at the Club with Ethan. Mitch had moved to a nearby table to flirt with one of the other members while he and Ethan drank, a lot. It was the only thing that kept him from remembering that look on Ellie's face.

"I hurt her," he mumbled into his beer. "I wanted to make her happy and instead I hurt her."

"Not your fault. She's the one judging you. It's a bullshit excuse to not be with you. She could figure out a way. Hell, you gave her a way but nooo, she won't do it." Ethan tossed back his shot.

"Yeah." Kind of. He'd spent a lot of time with Ethan lately and was used the other man mixing his own experience with Adrian's. It didn't matter. The two situations were close enough. "But I still hurt her. Her fault or not, she cried because of me."

"I refuse to think about that. Her tears are hers, not mine. She caused them." Ethan filled both of their shot glasses. "Women deserve to cry. They tear out our hearts through our dicks and then tell us it's our fault." He took a drink of his brandy. "Fuck them."

"That's the fun part." Damn, he was horny, but he didn't want any of these women. He wanted Ellie.

"Yeah, it is." Ethan sounded as wistful as he felt.

Adrian drank his shot, chasing it down with some beer. Ethan straightened in his chair, staring across the bar at one of the female members of the Club. She was older, probably in her forties and very attractive.

"You should go for it." He'd feel better if one of them got laid tonight.

"Her?" Ethan chuckled. "She'd chew me up and spit me out."

"No one refuses you." He sent the other guy a disgusted look. Women practically fainted when they saw him.

"She wouldn't refuse me. She'd lecture me and dice up my feelings into tiny pieces before stabbing each one with a toothpick and flicking it away." Ethan tossed back another shot. "I've seen Dale flirt with her for years. I don't know how the man stands being eviscerated so often."

"She seems nice." He'd seen her around the Club. She seemed to have a lot of friends here.

"She is. Polite. Educated. Beautiful. A fabulous person to talk to but if you flirt with her, she'll tear your heart out." Ethan stood. "Mine's already gone so she might turn me down. I've got nothing for her to feed on."

The woman noticed them staring and raised her glass.

Ethan nodded a hello. "I'm going to my office before she comes over to berate me. You're welcome to join me for cards and drinks."

"Sounds good." The two of them spent most nights in Ethan's office. Sometimes Mitch or one of Ethan's other friends would join them and those nights were fun. If it were only the two of them, they ended up bitching about women but since Ellie was all he thought about, that worked for him too.

Ethan's phone beeped. "One minute." He turned aside and answered it.

CHAPTER 26: ELLIE

"Membership." The bouncer stopped Ellie at the door to La Petite Mort Club.

"Ah…You remember me, don't you?" She'd thought she could smile and walk right in. They'd barely looked at the pass the last time. "I was here on Christmas. You escorted me to the stage for the Mistletoe Game."

"We were closed Christmas."

"Sorry. I meant Christmas Eve." She smiled.

"I need your membership, miss."

"That's why I'm here. I need to speak to Ethan." She'd rather find Adrian and tell him what she thought of his part in this but yelling at Ethan would be a start.

"Ethan's busy."

"How do you know?" The bouncer sure had been friendlier the last time.

"He's always busy." He looked over her shoulder. "Hey Richard, go on through."

"Why does he get to go inside without showing you his membership? Is it because he's a man?"

"It's because I've known Damon since the day he

started," said the older gentleman who the bouncer had called Richard.

"That's nice but how does he know you're still a member?"

Richard laughed. "That's a good question. Damon, how do you know my membership wasn't rescinded since last night?"

Damon was not amused. "Trust me. I would've heard." The bouncer looked at her. "Go away."

"That's no way to speak to a young lady," chided Richard.

"She's not a member."

"That's a real shame." Richard's blue-gray eyes roamed over her.

This man was her one chance to get through those doors. She stared up at him, trying to look helpless. "That's why I need to speak with Ethan. I want to talk to him about my membership."

"Please tell me you haven't caused trouble in here." Richard frowned. "Ethan isn't known to be forgiving in those situations."

"I haven't. I swear." That'd been Marc not her.

"Damon, can you call Ethan and have him come talk to this young lady?" Richard pulled out his wallet and handed the bouncer some money.

"You're going to get me fired." Damon took his phone from his pocket. "Ethan's been in a mood lately."

"Yes, he has, and she may be the distraction he needs." Richard's eyes roamed over her again. "She could distract me from many things." He smiled at her. "Good luck, miss?"

"Ellie."

"I hope to see you inside one day soon, Ellie." Richard walked into the Club.

"I can't bring her to your office," said Damon. "I'm the only one at the door. Jimmy isn't here yet. Yeah. Okay." He hung up the phone. "Ethan will be here in a minute." The line was getting long behind her. "Wait over there." He pointed to a chair on the other side of the double doors. It was shoved in the corner and was identical to the one Damon was sitting on. It was probably for that other bouncer Jimmy.

"Thank you." She smiled at his frown and walked to the chair. She peered into the Club. Adrian was at the bar alone. The restriction around her chest eased a bit. They weren't together. He could be with whomever he wanted but that didn't mean she was ready to see her replacement.

A group of three women passed her. She glanced at Damon. He was busy checking a man's membership card against his phone. She slipped off the chair and tagged along behind the women. She scanned the crowd. Ethan was talking to a couple, but his gaze kept darting toward the door. She moved to the other side of the women and prayed he wouldn't see her.

When they passed him, she made her way toward the bar. A woman now sat next to Adrian. He'd moved on. Good for him. She ignored the twisting of the knife in her heart. No matter how much she wanted him, she wasn't here to beg him to give her another chance. She was here to tell him that he had no right to try and stop her from moving on too.

CHAPTER 27: ADRIAN

Adrian searched the Club for someone who sparked his interest. He was tired of jerking off every night. His gaze landed on a couple, wearing masks and stepping onto one of the stages. They looked familiar but his mind was fuzzy from too much booze and not any food.

"I'll be right back," said Ethan. "There's something I have to deal with at the door."

"Sure. I'll be here." He had nowhere else to go. He watched as the man on stage tied the woman to a spanking bench. He should've spanked Ellie's ass more than he had. He'd never actually held her down over his lap and spanked her. He should've. He would've if he'd known he'd never get another chance to do anything with her.

The man lifted the woman's dress, exposing a nice ass and a sexy thong before her slapped her butt with a paddle.

"You like the show?" The woman Ethan had been watching pulled out a chair and sat on the seat next to him.

"It's okay." The man was teasing the woman now, caressing her ass, his hand slipping between her legs to touch softer places.

"I'm Cassandra." She held out her hand.

"Adrian." He shook it. Her skin was soft and her smile pretty but not as pretty as Ellie's.

"Have you heard their story?" She nodded at the stage.

"Their story? No."

"It's quite romantic."

"Really?" He didn't think of romance and this place.

"Yes. They only wear the masks when they're performing. It's in homage to the masquerade ball that saved Craig and Liz's marriage. They were on the verge of divorce—"

"Craig and Liz?" Why were those names so familiar?

"Yes," said Cassandra. "Are they friends of yours?"

Ellie stormed toward him.

"Not exactly." They weren't his friends; they were Ellie's parents.

CHAPTER 28: ELLIE

"I can't believe you convinced your friend to deny my membership." Ellie stopped in front of Adrian, ignoring the way her heart raced at the sight of him.

"Ah…Ellie. You shouldn't be here." Adrian kept glancing at the stage where a woman was getting paddled by a man in a mask.

Ellie flinched. That had to hurt. She wanted to rub her own ass. That woman's butt was red. She forced her eyes back to Adrian. "Too bad. I am. And you have no right trying to keep me from joining."

"What are you talking about?" He pulled his eyes away from the stage. "You know what? It doesn't matter. Let's get out of here." He stood.

"What?" She'd expected him to deny it or to argue with her.

"Let's go. You wanted to talk. Let's go talk." He grabbed her arm.

"No. Absolutely not. You've ignored me, my texts and my phone calls but now you want to talk. Why? What are you hiding?" She turned to the older woman who looked highly amused. "Hi, I'm Ellie. I used to live with this man but it's over. You're welcome to him, but I need to warn you that he seems really sweet, but he can be a controlling jerk." She sat next to the woman. "He's trying to keep me from joining this club."

"I am not." Adrian almost growled.

"Nice to meet you, Ellie. I'm Cassandra and thank you but even though he's gorgeous, I'm not interested."

"Ellie, please. We need to leave." Again, his eyes darted to the stage. The man was bent behind the woman, his face buried between her legs.

"I'd rather stay." She stared at the couple on stage. "I like to watch this stuff too and don't think that I'll care who you fuck because I won't." Those were the hardest words she'd ever said. She waved at the bartender. "I'll have a vodka and grapefruit."

"It's on me," said Cassandra.

"Thanks, but you don't have to do that." She didn't want the woman thinking that she was interested.

"I know I don't, but this is the most fun I've had in months"—she stared over Ellie's head for a moment—"and I have a feeling it's about to get better."

"You have no idea," muttered Adrian who was once again watching the stage where the man was untying the woman.

"You." Ethan stopped at Ellie's side.

She was pretty sure she literally gulped. The man really did look like a fallen angel, a very angry one.

"Yes?" Playing dumb was the best card she had right

now. "There you are. I was looking—"

"You were told to wait at the door."

"Oh…gee, I must've misunderstood."

"You didn't misunderstand you disobeyed."

"I'm not a dog." Her temper revved up a notch.

"Or apparently a sub." Cassandra laughed.

"Ethan, let's take this to your office." Adrian tipped his head toward the stage, his eyes on Ethan.

Why was Adrian so obsessed with that show? The couple wasn't even doing anything interesting anymore. They were walking off the stage, the woman tucked protectively against the masked man's side. Great, now she couldn't look away. He was so loving and caring. Ellie was jealous. It was obvious in every look and touch that the couple was deeply in love. It made Ellie's heart melt.

"You're right. We should go to my office." Ethan tapped her shoulder. "Come with me. Now."

"Fine." It was time to tell Adrian and Ethan exactly what she thought of them, but she didn't want to make a scene. She slid off the stool, her gaze drifting back to that couple. There was something familiar about them.

"Ellie." Adrian grabbed her arm, shifting her face toward him. "Let's go. Now."

She jerked free of his hold. She hated that even the slightest touch from him sent tingles racing through her body. "You don't get to order me around. Remember? I'm nothing to you now."

"I never said that. Never."

"You may as well have." It was clear in everything he

97

did—not answering her texts and phone calls. Not wanting to see her anymore. Everything.

"I'd never say that."

"Stop arguing and…oh fuck," mumbled Ethan.

"Ellie, is that you?"

Oh shit. Why was her mother here? She felt like a kid getting caught sneaking out of the house except this time she was in a sex club. She spun toward her mother's voice. "I can expl…"

The couple who'd been on stage stood there staring at her. The woman reached up and removed her mask.

Ellie's eyes almost popped out of her head. "Mom?" Her gaze landed on the man. "Dad? Oh my God."

"You're right. This has gotten much better," said Cassandra.

CHAPTER 29: ADRIAN

Adrian waited with Ellie upstairs at the Club. Ethan had ushered Craig and Liz to his office and them to one down the hallway.

"Do you want some water or something?" He walked over to a small fridge in the corner of the office.

"I want to go home." She sat on a chair staring down at her hands in her lap. She looked fragile like a broken doll or a small child.

"Okay. I'll go talk to your parents."

"No." She almost jumped from the chair. "I can't talk to them. Not right now."

"Ah…but you want to go home?" She wasn't making any sense.

She blinked and then wiped a large tear off her cheek. "Not to my parents' home. To your apartment." She tucked her feet up on the chair. "Is that okay?"

He wanted to wrap her in his arms and protect her from everything. "Of course. Give me a minute." He walked toward the door, but it opened before he could get there.

Ethan stepped inside the room. "Your parents are ready

to see you now."

"No. I can't." She shook her head, her eyes pleading with Adrian.

"Ethan, I'm going to take her home. They can talk tomorrow."

"Craig and Liz want to see her tonight."

"I'll talk to them," he said.

"I already did." Ethan's blue eyes landed on Ellie. "And they aren't thrilled about any of this. Their rights here have been violated."

"I violated *their* rights?" Ellie snorted.

"In this club they have a right to privacy."

"They were on stage."

"They have a right to their secrets, and you took that away from them when you trespassed. I should have you arrested."

"Hold on." He stepped in front of Ellie. "She didn't know."

"She was told to wait at the door." Ethan's tone was icy enough to freeze fire.

"She made a mistake."

"A costly one for both her and her parents."

"Ethan, please. Let me take her home. This isn't a good time for any of them to talk."

"That's up to Craig and Liz."

"And Ellie." He was getting tired of Ethan treating her like she didn't matter. Yes, it was her fault, but she was involved in this mess too.

"She's not my concern. She's not my customer."

"She's my concern and I'm taking her home." He grabbed her hand and pulled her to her feet.

Ethan shook his head, smiling slightly as two of his bouncers stepped into the doorway, making it clear that no one was leaving without Ethan's consent.

"Don't do this, Ethan. They can talk tomorrow."

Ethan studied them a moment before saying, "You leave here with her and your membership is terminated."

"I don't give a shit about my membership." Adrian relaxed. Ethan was letting them go.

"I hope you don't regret that decision." Ethan's gaze fell on Ellie.

"I won't." He did too. He liked hanging out with Ethan, but he had to take care of Ellie. She came first for him. "Come on, Ellie."

"Not so fast," said Ethan. "Craig and Liz expect to speak with their daughter tonight. If you can convince them to wait until tomorrow, the two of you may leave."

"I'll only be gone a minute." Adrian squeezed Ellie's hand. "Then I'll take you home."

CHAPTER 30: ELLIE

As soon as Adrian stepped out of the door, Ethan closed it and walked toward Ellie.

"The only reason I'm not calling the police is because of your parents and Adrian."

"I had no idea that—"

"You were told to stay at the door. You don't listen to anyone, do you?"

"I...I do." She wasn't that bullheaded.

Ethan's eyes roamed over her. "It's a shame Adrian isn't a true dominant. You could learn some valuable lessons as a sub."

"I..." Her eyes were probably bulging from her head.

"Not that he should waste his time with you, but he will." His face lost some of the anger. "Don't fuck it up. He's not your ex." Ethan turned and left the room.

CHAPTER 31: ADRIAN

Adrian made some tea and took it to Ellie. She'd been silent the entire trip back to their apartment. Now, she sat on the couch, clutching a pillow to her chest. Another pillow and a blanket were tossed in the corner of the sofa. She must've fallen asleep while watching TV last night.

"Here." He placed the tea on the end table next to her. "Come on. It's not that bad, is it?" He sat down by her. "Yes, they're your parents but you knew they had sex."

"I didn't know they went to a sex club." She gave him a disbelieving look, but it was better than her wounded child look.

"And they didn't know you did." He was trying to sympathize with her, but he was beginning to see the humor in the whole thing.

"I never got on a stage..."

He raised his brow, unable to keep the grin contained any longer.

"That was different. You didn't bare my ass and paddle me."

"No, but I buried my face between your legs." He took

her hand. "It'll be okay. They're embarrassed. You're embarrassed. Just talk to them."

"I will." She dropped her head onto the back of the couch and sighed. "When are they coming over?"

"Tomorrow around noon." He stood. "Are you hungry? I can order take out or something."

"No. I want to go to bed."

"It's only nine o'clock."

"I know but I just want this day to be done." She stuffed the pillow on the end of the sofa next to the other one.

"Okay, good night." He plopped back down on the couch, reaching for the remote.

"Oh. Right. I'll sleep in the other room." She gathered the pillows and the blanket.

"Have you been sleeping on the couch?"

"Yeah." She wouldn't meet his eyes.

"Why?" He swore he could hear his heart thudding in his chest.

"Too lonely in that room." She pointed to her room. "And too many memories in yours."

Some of the pieces of his heart that she'd shattered started to bind together with hope, but he couldn't go through this again. "Oh. Okay. I'll go to my room then." He knew he sounded less than thrilled but he didn't want those memories haunting his dreams either.

"No. I'll sleep in the other room so you can watch TV."

"You sure?" He almost sighed with relief. He hadn't

been looking forward to being locked in that room from now until morning with nothing to do but think.

"Yeah. Goodnight, Adrian." She handed him one of the pillows. "Here. You'll need this. I stole it from your bed."

"No, that's fine. I only use the one anyway."

"It's the one you use." Again, she wouldn't meet his eyes.

"You've been sleeping with my pillow?" Another piece of his heart started to cling to the others.

"I like the smell of your cologne."

"Oh." Was that it or did it mean something more? He handed it back to her. "You can keep it. I'll use a different one." If she had his pillow, then the one she used was probably still in his bed.

"Are you sure?"

"Yeah." He stared at her, hoping she'd say something else.

She sat there for what seemed like forever before saying, "Goodnight." She stood and started for her room.

That was it then. He wasn't chasing after her. He leaned back against the couch and pointed the remote at the TV. The Valentine's gift that he'd bought her sat next to the television. He didn't even think, the words just slipped from his mouth. "You never opened your gift."

She stopped and turned back toward him. "I figured you'd want to return it."

"Oh." He flipped through the channels not seeing anything as all those pieces of his heart shattered again.

He'd thought...no, hoped that she'd waited to open it because she'd wanted him to be there or perhaps, she was keeping it around to remind her of him. Instead, it was just Ellie trying not to take advantage of him. He'd spent weeks in a relationship with her and she considered it just a fuck fest.

CHAPTER 32: ELLIE

Ellie couldn't move. Until a second ago, she'd had a reason to hope that Adrian still felt something for her. He'd been warm and kind but now, he was distant. He was only sitting a few feet from her, but it seemed like he was miles away. She had to fix this. "Do you want me to open it?"

"I don't care." He turned toward her. "I won't be returning it, so you don't have to worry about that. I didn't spend much. It's a stupid gift." He walked over and picked it up. "I'll just trash it."

"No, don't do that." She hurried over to him. "Please."

"Really, it's stupid. I don't think you'll even want it."

"I do." She held out her hand.

"I never should've mentioned it." He gave it to her before sitting back down on the couch. "I'm telling you. You're going to think it's stupid."

"I won't." She sat next to him, putting the pillow between them. "It's from you. I'll"—her eyes met his—"love it."

His gaze dropped to her lips and she leaned toward him. She wanted to touch him, kiss him, make love with him. He leaned in, his breath teasing across her lips and then he turned away.

"Sor…" She cleared her throat, trying not to cry. "Sorry." She stood. "Goodnight."

"Wait." He stared up at her, his green eyes sad. "It's not that I don't want to but…I don't think I can do this. Nothing has changed between us and I can't be with someone who doesn't trust me."

"I do trust you or at least I'm trying." Ellie had to convince him because she couldn't lose him. "I know you didn't sleep with anyone on Valentine's Day. I believe you."

"You still think I'm like Marc."

"I don't. I swear."

"What about tonight?"

"Tonight?" She had no idea what he was talking about.

"You thought I'd stop you from becoming a member of the Club because we weren't together."

"What was I supposed to think?"

"Gee, Ellie, anything but blaming me would be a start. Why would I do that? This proves that you still think I'm an ass."

"You don't understand. Wait. Give me a minute." She hurried into her room and grabbed the letter from her purse. She walked back into the living room and handed it to him. "What would you think? I had no idea…I never would've dreamed that my parents were the conflict of interest." She shuddered. "I still don't want to believe it." She sat on the couch. "You're the only one who I know…knew who's a member."

"What about Marc?" He put the paper down on the coffee table.

"He's not a member. He spent all week after Christmas bitching about how Ethan had told him that he'd never be a member."

"Oh…I guess I can see your point on this one, even though I'd never do something like that."

"I know but I knew you hated me and—"

"I don't hate you. I could never hate you." His green eyes softened.

"Really?" She was making some headway.

"Yeah." His gaze slipped to her lips and then he blinked, the softness gone from his eyes. "What did you think I was doing at the Club?"

"Ah." Shit, there went her headway.

"I want the truth, Ellie. No lies."

"It's a sex club, Adrian."

"I know what it is. What I don't know is what you think I do when I'm there."

"Have sex. Okay." She had to make him see that this time was different. "But I wasn't mad. Sure, I was hurt but not mad. We weren't together anymore. I didn't expect you to be celibate."

"Were you celibate?"

"Of course."

"Then why would you think I wouldn't be?"

"Because you're a guy."

"A guy. Any guy or a guy like me?" His words had an

edge of hurt to them.

"Any guy but being extremely good looking and funny and charming does increase your odds of success."

His lips twitched a little and Ellie's hope grew.

"I guess, I'll have to concede that point too."

"I don't know what else to do to prove to you that I trust you."

"I don't know either." The sparkle in his eyes died.

That wasn't what she'd wanted to hear but it wasn't a no either.

"Let me sleep on it."

"Sure. That's fair." She didn't like it but again it wasn't a no. She stood.

"Do you want to watch some TV?"

"I'd like that." That little hope was multiplying fast. "You want some popcorn?"

"Yeah. I'm starving."

"I'll make a huge bowl." She hurried into the kitchen. This wasn't much but it was a start and she'd take it.

CHAPTER 33: ADRIAN

Adrian turned off the TV. Ellie was asleep on the other end of the couch, curled into a tiny ball, like she didn't want to be noticed. As if he'd ever not notice her. From the moment he'd seen her she'd been the only one he'd noticed.

He was pretty sure he'd still be wanting her on his death bed. He'd definitely want her by his side, holding his hand when he took his last breath. He stood and pulled her covers over her shoulder before brushing the hair from the side of her face. She murmured in her sleep, turning into his hand.

"Fuck, Ellie. I'm in love with you and it's killing me." He bent and kissed her forehead before walking to his room. He flipped on the light and stared at his bed. It'd never seemed so big and empty. Who was he kidding? He was going to give her...give them another chance. She'd said she'd try and that was all he could ask. He wasn't perfect either. He should tell her now and stop torturing them both.

He walked back to the couch and stood there, watching her sleep. She looked so peaceful. He couldn't wake her. She'd had a shit day and by the dark circles under her eyes, she hadn't been sleeping much. He could tell her tomorrow but damn it, he was sleeping with her tonight. He picked her up and carried her to his room…no, their room. He gently placed her on her side of the bed, tucking the covers around her before going into the living room and grabbing his pillow. He inhaled as he walked back to their bedroom. It smelled more like her than him and that was perfect.

He stretched out on his side and watched her sleep. He was going to make this work. He had to. She owned his heart and he'd already lived too long without it.

CHAPTER 34: ELLIE

Ellie woke feeling better than she had in a long time. She'd actually slept like the dead. She stretched and rolled over. That wasn't right. If she rolled over on the couch she'd be on the floor and she definitely wasn't on the floor. She bounced up like a spring. She was in Adrian's bed.

She turned, hoping to see his large body stretched out next to hers but the bed was empty. Had he slept with her? Had he forgiven her? Did this mean they were starting again? She had a hundred questions and no one to answer them.

His side looked like it'd been slept in but there was one way to know for sure. She leaned over, putting her face in his pillow and inhaling. It smelled of him. The scent clean and fresh. She wrapped her arms around the pillow and buried her face in the softness. He'd slept on this pillow, with her, in his bed. No, it was their bed in their room in their apartment. She jumped up and hurried out of the room.

"Hey." He was at the table working on his laptop.

"Hey." Suddenly, she was nervous. What if last night

had been nothing more than two friends sharing a bed?

"I picked up some sandwiches and a fruit and veggie tray from the store."

"You've been to the store already?" She glanced out the window. The sun was high in the sky.

"Yeah, and to the gym." His eyes roamed over her, heating her blood. "I had a hard time sleeping."

"Oh, did I snore?" She was pretty sure his hard time had to do with that lovely appendage between his legs and she was more than happy to help him with that.

"No"—his eyes darkened—"but we can talk about that later."

"Later?" Did that mean they weren't together? Adrian never suggested putting sex off until later.

"Your parents are going to be here soon."

"Oh, shoot. What time is it?" She'd forgotten all about that and what'd happened yesterday. She shuddered at the memory.

He looked at the computer. "Eleven twenty."

"And they'll be here at noon?" She hadn't meant for her voice to sound so shrill but that was only forty minutes away.

"Yeah,"

"Why didn't you wake me?"

"I was going to at eleven thirty."

"A half hour. You were going to give me only a half hour to get ready? Argh. You're such a man."

"That didn't sound like a compliment," he hollered as she hurried to her bathroom.

Damn, she was screwing this up already. She stopped, turning toward him. "I didn't mean—"

"I know. I was joking." His eyes sparkled with humor.

"Oh." Her heart started beating again. "I better shower." She stepped into her bathroom and opened the shower curtain. She touched the knob but didn't turn on the water. He'd made the first gesture by putting her in bed with him. She was going to make the next one. She grabbed her towel, shampoo and other things from the bathroom and hurried across the house.

He sat at the table and watched her, not saying a word. She was going to take his silence and unreadable expression as happiness. If it were something else, he'd have to tell her to move her things back to the other bathroom.

CHAPTER 35: ADRIAN

Adrian answered the door. Ellie's parents were early. "Hi, come in." He stepped aside. "Ellie's still in the shower. She should be out shortly."

Craig looked at him, eyes narrowed. Adrian was glad he'd showered hours before and his hair was dry because Craig was sizing him up with his dad-eyes.

"Please have a seat." He pointed to the table where he'd put the food. "Would you like something to drink? We have Coke, water, orange juice."

"Water, please," said Liz as she sat. "This looks delicious but I'm not very hungry." Her face was pale and there were dark circles under her eyes.

He felt bad for them and for Ellie. This wasn't going to be an easy thing to get past. He put three bottles of water on the table as Ellie stepped out of their bedroom. She wore jeans and a T-shirt. Her hair was still wet, and she hadn't put on makeup. She looked like a teenager who was about to get into trouble for staying out all night. Nothing could've stopped him from walking over to her and taking her hand in his.

She looked up at him with gratitude.

"Ellie," said her father, his voice gruff.

"Dad. Mom." She walked to the table, pulling Adrian with her.

He gave her hand a squeeze. "I'm going to head out. I'll be back in…a few hours?" He looked around the table.

"No. Stay." She tightened her grip.

"Ah…It's probably best if I go." He appreciated that she wanted him with her, but this was going to be an awkward conversation as it was. His presence would only make it worse.

"He's right," said her mother. "Go and take Craig."

"What?" Ellie looked at her mom.

Craig jumped up like he'd been freed from a trap. He kissed Liz on the cheek and said, "Call when this is…when you're ready."

"I will and you owe me one." Liz smiled slightly at her husband.

"Anything." He almost ran to the door.

Adrian looked at Ellie. He had to make sure she was okay with this. She nodded. He wanted to run to the door too but instead he gave her hand one last squeeze and calmly walked to the door.

"Where are we going?" asked Craig as they walked out of the apartment.

"I was meeting some friends for pool at Murphy's."

"Sounds great." Craig followed him to the parking lot. "You drive. Liz can pick me up later."

"You aren't coming back here?" He opened his car and

got in the driver's seat.

"Not if I don't have to. Right now, I don't want to see my daughter."

"This isn't her fault."

"Her fault? No, but it wasn't easy seeing her there." Craig gave Adrian a hard look. "And it's not easy knowing that the baby girl whose diapers you changed is with a man who's a member of La Petite Mort Club."

Suddenly, he wanted to run back into the apartment. "I don't go there much."

"Right. I've seen you there. I didn't recognize you at first but once I did, I know who you are."

Good God, it was hot in this car. "I...I've never taken Ellie there."

"Keep it that way."

"I will." He had no choice not after last night.

Craig huffed. "I should also tell you that as much as I hate this, my wife is going to tell Ellie that you and she can have the even number months and she and I will have the odd number months." He turned to Adrian. "I mean this as seriously as a gun to your head. If you're there at midnight on the last day of the month, get out. I don't ever, ever want to see my daughter in that place again."

"Yes, sir." This was serious but he was about to burst out laughing. "I have to say I don't think she ever wants to see you there either."

Silence filled the car. Shit. He'd gone too far. He really had to control his jokes. Not everyone found this shit amusing.

"I have no doubt about that." Craig chuckled. "It isn't something you want to see your parents doing." He dropped his head in his hands. "Fuck, that was horrible for all of us."

"Yeah, but kind of funny now that it's over." He cringed, glancing at Ellie's father. "Too soon?"

"Yeah, too soon." Craig glared at him. "And let me be clear. In a hundred years, it'll still be too soon."

"Sorry." He wasn't. It was funny. He didn't like Ellie being upset but this was funny.

"One more thing and my wife has no say about this at all."

Uh-oh. Here it came.

"I don't like the idea of my daughter at a place like that, but I can accept it if, and only if, she's there with a man who loves her. Understand?"

"Yes, sir." He did. Completely.

"Good but I'm gonna spell it out for you anyway. I don't care if the women agree that you get the even number months. Do not take her there unless you're going to protect her, watch over her and love her. Got it."

"I got it, sir but you don't have to worry. I'm not even a member anymore."

"Oh, Ethan wasn't serious. He was trying to show Ellie that you'd choose her over the Club. Ethan may seem like a hard-ass and he's been grumpy as hell lately but he's a romantic at heart. He saved my marriage. Without his help I think we would've gotten divorced."

"Ethan helped?" He'd never imagined the man as a

119

matchmaker.

"Yeah. So, the question, that you seem to be avoiding, is do you love her?"

He glanced at Ellie's dad. "I'm afraid I do, sir. Actually, I'm terrified, sir." He didn't like being this vulnerable. It went against his nature but there was nothing he could do about it now.

Craig laughed. "Glad to hear it and yeah, it's terrifying but it's also the best feeling in the world."

He nodded. He was sure Craig was right but only if she loved him back. Otherwise, it was the worst feeling in the world.

CHAPTER 36: ELLIE

Ellie fidgeted with her water bottle. She was glad her dad was gone but she wished Adrian were here. He'd been right to leave but she still wanted him by her side.

"This is quite embarrassing for all of us. Your poor father…Let's just say he's not handling this too well."

"It's okay, Mom. I understand. You're both adults. You can do what you want but please let's not talk about it."

"I think we need to."

"I really don't want to." She rather have a tooth pulled with no anesthesia than talk about her parents' kinky sex life.

"And neither do I but I learned that it's important to discuss things. Lack of communication almost cost me my marriage."

"We're not married."

Her mom made a face at her. "I know that, but I don't want you avoiding us because of this."

"I won't." She might but only for a while…until she could forget seeing her mother's ass cherry red from her father spanking it. It'd probably take a few decades but then she'd visit them again.

"I don't believe you. Out of our three kids, you've always been the most uptight about sex."

"Me? Uptight about sex?" She liked sex. She loved it with Adrian. She wasn't uptight.

"Yes, darling. You. You're so uncomfortable talking about it, that I've often wondered if you believe you and your siblings were some kind of miraculous conception." Mom laughed.

"Hardly. I know you and Dad have sex, but I don't want to talk about it." She met her mom's eyes for the first time. "And I definitely don't want to see it."

"Yes. That was a bit awkward." Mom's eyes gleamed with humor. "You're actually lucky. We don't have sex in public. We just play a bit."

"And that was more than enough for me." She wanted to scrape those images from her head—Mom's pink ass in the air and the sounds, the paddle hitting flesh, the moans of pleasure. "How could you...like that?"

Mom shrugged. "I don't know. I'd never imagined anything like that, but when your father and I saw another couple....we decided to try it. It saved our marriage. All of it. That place. The variations in our sex life."

She wanted to put her hands over her ears and sing the ABC's or something, but she was also fascinated. It was like a car accident. She didn't want to know but she had to look.

"Remember I told you about how we almost got

divorced. It was because I found a membership to La Petite Mort Club in your dad's belongings. We hadn't been intimate in a while and I thought...No, I knew it was because he was going there. Instead of asking him, I blamed him and kicked him out."

"Had he been going there? Cheating on you?"

"No."

"How do you know for sure?" How would she ever know for sure about Adrian?

"Because he told me, and I believe him. I trust him." Mom dipped a carrot stick into the ranch dressing and took a bite. "You can't be with someone 24/7 so you have to trust them." She finished the carrot. "How are things between you and Adrian?"

Ellie felt the tears run down her cheeks. "I'm in love with him, Mom. I think he's willing to give me another chance but what if I blow that? What if I can't prove to him that I do trust him and...and..."

"Ellie, if you love him, don't let your past ruin your future. From everything I've seen Adrian truly cares for you...loves you."

"Do you think so?" She shook her head. "No. I don't know."

"Trust me. No man drives you all the way home on Christmas, let's you move into his apartment and is willing to give up his membership to La Petite Mort Club for a woman unless he's in love."

"You heard about him giving up his membership?"

"Ethan told us. He was worried your father wouldn't

be too happy about seeing his daughter at a sex club."
Mom's lips twitched. "He was right."

"You guys were there too and I'm an adult."

"You're still our baby. You'll always be our baby."
Mom took her hand. "You'll understand when you have
kids."

That'd never happen at the rate she was going with
relationships. "How do I not screw this up?"

"Let him know that you trust him." Mom's face heated
slightly. "Many men like to be in control. They don't
always get that in their day-to-day life. They aren't the boss
at work or often, at home. I know I can be a bit of a take-
charge kind of woman and you're a lot like me."

That was true. She tended to be a bit bossy sometimes.

"Let him know that you need him. Trust him." Mom's
cheeks turned a little brighter. "One way of doing that is in
bed or on stage." Her eyes darted to her daughter's and she
smiled wistfully. "Afterwards is always lovely. You hold
each other. You feel so connected. It's a great time to talk
and share all those secrets you're normally afraid to say out
loud."

"I don't think I'm ready to get tied up on stage." Tied
up by Adrian in their bed was a different story.

"And that's fine, but I'm sure you can think of
something else he might like. Men aren't hard to please in
the bedroom."

She wasn't ready to let him hit her with a paddle; she
may never be. However, she'd liked it when he'd slapped
her ass. She'd also enjoyed tying him up. She could let him

tie her up. That'd show trust or…That was it. She knew exactly what she was going to do. "Mom, I think we should meet them at Murphy's and play pool."

CHAPTER 37: ADRIAN

Adrian was having a good time with Craig. The man had a great sense of humor and was excellent at pool.

"Damn Adrian, you brought in a ringer." Mitch waved at the waitress. "I got this round, but you guys will lose the next one and then you're buying." He racked the balls.

"Sorry, but I'm going to have to sit out the next game." Craig put his stick down.

Adrian started to ask why but his words tangled in his throat as he followed Craig's gaze. Ellie and Liz walked into the bar. They were gorgeous, both smiling and laughing. He couldn't pull his eyes away. He'd never seen Ellie so happy and relaxed. A stab of jealousy dug into his heart. He wanted to be the one to make her that happy.

Her eyes found his and her smiled widened, wiping away that jealousy like it was nothing more than a fleck of dust. He put his pool stick down. "I'm out too."

"I guess it's just us," said Mitch to Derek and Sonny.

"Nope. Count me out," said Derek. "I need to get home."

"Pussy-whipped," said Sonny.

"Yep and loving every minute of it." Derek walked to the bar to pay his tab.

"Let's head to the Club," said Sonny.

"Sounds good to me." Mitch waved. "Adios, fellas and ladies." He winked at Ellie as he and Sonny left.

"Everything good?" Craig looked nervous as his wife and daughter approached him.

"Perfect." Liz kissed him. "Have you been cleaning these poor boys out of their beer money?"

"Of course." Craig's hands rested on her waist.

"Then it's about time you lose." Liz turned to Ellie. "How about girls against boys?"

"Sounds good to me," said Ellie.

"You play?" he asked as Ellie stopped by his side. "Sometimes."

"How come you never played when we were here?"

"You never asked." She took his hand. "It's okay though because Alison was here, and she doesn't play." She wrinkled her nose. "She's not very good."

"Then let's play but first, what would you ladies like to drink?"

"Lite beer on tap." Liz was busy checking out the pool table.

"Same for me," said Ellie.

"Is your mom a professional or something?"

"No." Ellie laughed as she followed Adrian to the bar. "But she's good and she's very competitive and so am I." Ellie shrugged. "That's another reason I seldom play. When I do, I play to win. I usually beat the guys I'm playing

127

against and that never sits well with alpha-cavemen." She looked up at him. "But you're different."

"I am." He bent, slowly moving in for a kiss and giving her every opportunity to step away. She leaned forward, meeting him halfway. The kiss was a sweet touching of the lips. He wanted to grab her and press her against his body while he devoured her, but her father must be watching. He leaned away, unable to wipe the smile from his face. "Everything go ok with your mom?"

"Excellent. I even have a surprise for you."

"You do? I like surprises." Maybe she was wearing some sexy undies or something. He tugged the bottom of her T-shirt letting his knuckles rub her belly. "Is it something you're going to show me in private?

"Yep, I'll even let you take it out of me if you ask nicely."

His dick had begun to wake when he'd seen her, but it was wide awake now. "Take it out of you?"

"That's what I said." She reached around him and pulled his phone from his back pocket. She scrolled through and tapped something and then handed it to him.

The app for the sex toy was activated. "No." He shook his head.

"Yes." She nodded.

He lowered his voice as his dick rose. "You're telling me that you have that inside you. Now. With your parents here?" His eyes darted to Craig who was watching them, until Liz captured his attention.

"I trust you," said Ellie.

Liz smiled at them over Craig's shoulder.

"Does your mom know?"

"No. Do you want me to tell her?" Ellie gave him an odd look.

"No. God no."

"You sure?" She tried not to grin but failed miserably. "She may not mind. She told me that men like to be in charge."

"I don't have to be in charge." But he did like it.

"So, you don't want to tie me up and spank me?" She blinked innocently at him.

"Well, I didn't say that." If his dick had been awake before, now it'd just had an expresso.

"Do you want to do that?"

"Only if you want to but can we talk about this later? Your dad is already looking at me like he's about to dismember me and I have a good idea what he'd cut off first."

She laughed. "Dad will behave. Mom will take care of him." She stood on tiptoe and whispered in his ear, "Just like I'm going to take care of you."

"You're killing me, Ellie."

CHAPTER 38: ADRIAN

Adrian's hand itched to press the button on his phone. He and Craig were getting annihilated by the women in pool.

Ellie walked around the table looking for her next shot. He pulled his phone from his pocket, waving it at her. Her eyes widened for a moment and then she smiled. She knew he wouldn't use it, and that made him feel like he could conquer the world. She took her shot, making it and then the next.

"How in the hell are they this good?" he asked Craig.

"Sorcery." Craig laughed. "Seriously, I have no idea. Liz was a ringer when I met her."

"And she taught Ellie." It made sense.

"I guess. We have a table, but I don't remember them playing that much. Must be genetic."

He nodded, barely listening. His focus had shifted to Ellie's ass as she bent to take her next shot.

"Perhaps if you paid more attention to the game and less to my daughter's butt we wouldn't be losing so badly."

"Oh…shit. Sorry." He pulled his eyes away.

Craig laughed. "You can look but don't touch."

"Ah…yes, sir." Oh, he was so going to touch—and kiss and lick and…

"I'm her father." Craig frowned at him. "Learn to lie a little better than that." He walked over to Liz who was sitting at their table.

Ellie finished the game by landing the eight ball.

"It's time for us to call it a night." Liz stood as Craig pulled out his wallet.

"I've got it." Adrian waved the waitress over.

"Thanks, but this is on me." Craig handed the waitress his credit card.

"Thank you, Daddy." Ellie hugged him. "I love you."

"I love you too baby."

Her mom hugged her next. "You two have fun tonight."

"Liz, I don't want to hear it." Craig signed the receipt and handed it back to the waitress.

"What did I say?" asked Liz.

"I'm not stupid." Craig frowned at her.

"I never said you were." Liz kissed him. "I just told them to have fun. You need to get your mind out of the gutter."

"But you like it in the gutter," he mumbled quietly but not quietly enough.

"Dad, stop." Elle put her hands over her ears.

"Good night." Liz laughed, wrapping her arm through her husband's and dragging him to the door.

"So…" His eyes raked over Ellie. They were alone,

finally, kind of. The bar was more crowded than earlier, but her parents were gone. That was alone enough for him.

"Another game?" She racked the balls. "I'll give you five free shots."

"Ouch. I'm not that bad."

"No, but I'm that good."

"You certainly are, but I have a feeling this game is going to be different." He held up his phone.

"That'd be cheating." Her breath caught for a minute. "I didn't mean…"

"I know what you meant." He captured her chin and leaned down. He kissed her softly but this time he slid his tongue into her mouth for a quick taste. She was like a drug. One taste wasn't enough. He tightened his grip on her chin, holding her in place as he deepened the kiss. She melted against him. He had to stop before he pulled her into the bathroom for a quickie. He broke away, keeping his hold on her face. "I should take you home and fuck you senseless."

"Sounds good to me." She was slightly breathless, and he wanted to point out to everyone that he'd done this to her with nothing but a kiss.

"Tempting, but you've had that toy inside you all night while I had to stand here pretending that I didn't know and wondering how you felt having your pussy full. Did it move when you bent? Did it feel good? Make you horny? Are you wet right now?"

"Do you want answers?" Her breath was ragged.

"No. Now, we're going to play another game of pool

and I want you to remember that all's fair in love and war."
He grinned. "And this is war." He gave her another kiss,
this one harder and deeper. When he stepped back, they
were both panting, and he was about to make her pant
harder with nothing more than a touch of a button.

CHAPTER 39: ELLIE

Ellie missed another shot. "Damn it, that's not fair."

"What? I didn't do anything." Adrian stood on the other side of the pool table holding his phone.

"You need to give me the phone because I can't concentrate when you have it." She walked toward him with her hand out.

"Nope. Not gonna happen." He tapped the phone.

A vibration shot through her pussy. She stopped, clenching her thighs together.

"Hello." His voice was amused. "Did you like that?" He grinned. "I think you did." He tapped the phone again.

Another vibration pulsed inside her and she grasped the nearby table, biting her lip as her body tightened around the toy. Shit. It felt so damn good and then the vibrations stopped.

"So?" He watched her intently.

"Wow. That was surprising."

"How? Too much? Not enough?"

"No." She glanced around to make sure no one was close. "I've used them before, but this is different."

"Different good or different bad?" He studied his phone. "I haven't played with this app yet. There are a ton of settings. Intensity. Duration." He glanced up at her, grinning. "We can even save patterns, but you have to tell me what you like."

"It's different because"—she walked closer to him, lowering her voice. "I wasn't prepared. I didn't expect...Oh god."

He tapped his phone again, this time slowly sliding his finger up the screen, causing the vibrations to increase in intensity.

The damn thing was pressing right against her G-spot and she was about to climb the walls. She grabbed his arm. "Oh, god. Stop."

He slid his finger down and the vibrations subsided but it still hummed softly inside her.

"It's still on." She wasn't going to come but every cell in her body was focused on her pussy.

"I know." He smiled. "It's time for me to win a game." He locked the screen on his phone, slid it into his pocket and picked up his pool stick.

"This...is"—she squeezed her legs together—"cheating."

He walked around the table, looking for his shot. "No, this is war, baby." He looked at her. "Sorry. I didn't mean to call you baby."

"I don't mind when you're joking like that."

"Who's joking?" He lined up a shot and made it. "This is war. I can't let you win all night. I'd never hear the end of it when you tell my friends." He shot again but this time missed. "Your shot." He patted her ass as he walked by. "I've been wanting to do that all night."

"Why didn't you?" She grabbed her stick and walked around the table.

"Because I didn't want your father to punch me in the face."

"Dad wouldn't do that." She laughed.

"You're his baby girl and I'm the guy who's defiling her."

"Defiling? Now there's a word I haven't heard in years. Decades maybe." She lined up her shot.

He tapped his phone.

"Adrian." She dropped her stick and clasped onto the table. It was pulsing inside her, hard and strong. His finger skimmed along his screen and the intensity increased. She gasped for breath, her eyes locking with his. She was going to come right here if he didn't stop. She was a mess. Part of her wanted him to turn it off but the other part would weep if he did.

He touched the phone again and the vibrations slowed as he walked over to her, taking her hand. "I think we should go." The gruffness in his voice almost sent her over the edge, making her fingernails dig into his skin.

"Breathe"—he bent by her ear and whispered—"but do not come."

She nodded.

"I think we need to play with this at home before we try it in public again."

"Yes." She loved that idea.

CHAPTER 40: ADRIAN

Adrian had never seen a more beautiful sight than Ellie almost climaxing at the pool table. If they'd been alone or the bar had been a little more crowded and he'd been closer, he'd have let her come.

He held the car door for her and then got into the driver's seat. "You okay?"

"Yeah." She smiled at him. "I've got it under control."

"We can't have that because my dick's harder than a brick." He pulled out his phone as he started the car.

"No. Adrian, don't."

"I want you on edge all the way home." He opened the app and tapped the button.

"Adrian, plea…" She squeezed her legs together. "Shit. That feels so good."

The wiggle of her hips made him almost come in his pants. He pulled out of the parking lot. Thank god his place wasn't far away. "Next time, I'm going to stand behind you, holding you close so you can feel my dick against your ass. You're going to be so hot and so horny and I'm going to let you come at the bar. You'll have to be quiet or everyone will hear. Do you think you can do that?"

"I-I don't know." She rolled her hips and he wanted to be inside her when she did that, feel her body rock on his.

"If you don't everyone will hear you. They'll know what you did. I'll have my arms around you. I'll let you watch me turn up the intensity." He tapped the phone and increased the vibrations.

"Adrian, that's…" She moaned softly.

"What is it, Ellie? Tell me." He needed her to focus on him, on speaking, on anything but coming.

"Good. Really good."

He had to touch her. He pulled the car into the parking lot and reached over, grabbing her by the back of the neck and kissing her. It was hard and desperate just like his dick. His tongue invaded her mouth, and she wrapped her arms around his neck, kissing him back like he was the only thing in this world that mattered.

"Upstairs. Now." He pulled away and got out of the car.

She didn't wait for him to open her door. She almost jumped out of the car and raced up the steps. He took two at a time. As soon as he caught up to her, he swooped her off her feet, her back to his front, and lunged up the stairs. She leaned into him, her hands on his arms. His hand went between her legs and she groaned, her hips gyrating against his fingers. She was hot and ready.

"Foreplay is done." He unlocked the door, shoving it open.

CHAPTER 41: ELLIE

As soon as Adrian shut the door Ellie jumped him, literally. The vibrator still hummed inside her, but she needed real contact. She needed Adrian. She turned, throwing her arms around his neck and almost climbing up his body. She wrapped her legs around his thighs, his dick pressing against her belly.

He stumbled backward into the door, but his hands grabbed her ass lifting her. She moaned into his mouth as his erection rubbed against her clit. The vibrations pulsed inside her, but they weren't doing anything for her clit. She rocked against him, tearing at his shirt as he staggered to their bedroom.

He dropped her on the bed. "Take off your clothes."

She'd already begun pulling off her shoes. He tugged his shirt over his head as she kicked off her pants. They couldn't get naked fast enough. He unbuttoned his jeans, and she had to help. It'd been too long since she'd touched him. She pulled down his zipper, her hand grazing along his dick as she kissed his abdomen. He was so hot and strong. She pushed his pants and underwear down before wrapping her fingers around his cock and squeezing.

"Fuck, Ellie." He grabbed her head, but he didn't stop her. "I don't know if I…"

She didn't care. Right now, the only thing she cared about was tasting him, pleasing him. She licked up his length before sliding his dick into her mouth.

"Yes." He gasped.

She sucked harder, loving the tangy taste of his precum. She stroked his length with one hand as the other cupped his balls.

"Stop, babe. Ellie. I can't." He wrapped his hand in her hair and tugged her away from his cock. "I'm gonna come."

She stared up at him, taking one last lick along his tip before he pushed her back onto the bed. His face was hard with passion as his mouth found hers. His kiss was desperate and rough. He shoved her legs apart, sliding his dick through her slick folds. He was hot and hard and she needed him inside her.

"You feel so good." He stroked along her seam. "Fuck. I can feel the vibrations." He rested his cock against her opening, against the toy and moaned in her ear. "I'm gonna fuck your ass one day with this inside your pussy."

"Yes." She wrapped her arms around him, her body trembling at the thought. "Soon. We should do that soon."

He kissed her hard, his mouth devouring as he reached between her legs. She moaned as her body clung to the vibrator as he removed it, tossing it aside.

"Hurry." Her pussy clenched, looking for something to

cling to. She needed him inside her now.

He leaned over, fumbling with the drawer of the nightstand, searching for a condom. She kissed his neck, his shoulders, his chest—anywhere she could reach as her hands skimmed along his back and arms. She didn't ever want to let him go again. He tore open the condom and rolled it down his cock.

He grabbed her face, staring into her eyes as he slowly slid inside her, stretching her body and making her feel every inch. She squeezed his dick, keeping him close as she lost herself in his forest green eyes.

CHAPTER 42: ADRIAN

Adrian slid into Ellie, his balls already at the breaking point. She was hot and tight and perfect. He took his time, fucking her slowly and savoring every sensation, every sound—her soft moans, the way she tightened around his cock, her breath hitching as he pushed deeper. Her breasts rubbed against his chest, but she hadn't taken off her shirt. He needed to feel her skin on his. He shoved her shirt and bra out of his way, exposing her tits. He arched his back, burying himself deeper inside her and groaned as her nipples rubbed against his chest. He thrust fast and hard. Her eyes drifted shut.

He grabbed her face. "Look at me."

Her eyes fluttered open and he pulled almost all the way out, staring into her brown eyes as he slowly slid back inside her.

"Oh, oh, Adrian." Her legs wrapped around his calves, and her hips rocked, meeting his thrusts. She was so tight and so close to coming that her body trembled. He kept ahold of her face, daring her to look away or to close her eyes. Her gaze grew unfocused as he increased his pace, fucking her faster. Her fingers dug into his arms. She was close. He thrust into her over and over, faster and faster. She gasped, her body tightening around his cock as she came, her hips rocking with her release.

He gritted his teeth, trying to hold back his orgasm. He'd waited too long to get back inside her. He wasn't ready for it to be done. He slowed his pace, backing away from his release. He rode her orgasm, feeling her body softening under his. She was slipping into that zone of satiation and he wasn't letting that happen either. He pumped into her hard and fast, his dick barely withdrawing before he rocked back inside.

"Adrian, please." Her nails dug into his shoulder as her body, once relaxing began to stiffen again. He was taking her back up that mountain and this time they were coming together. He reached between them, his fingers dancing through her wetness and over her clit, rubbing fast and hard as his hips pumped into her over and over.

"Please, I can't...I..." She screamed, her body shattering and taking him with her. He slammed into her and grunted, his hips thrusting slower now, emptying his balls. He dropped onto her, his face buried in her neck, unable to move. "Fuck. I love you, Ellie." Unfortunately, he was still able to speak.

CHAPTER 43: ELLIE

Ellie's head rested on Adrian's chest. His words echoing through her heart. She wanted him to have meant what he said, but she knew it was just something that sometimes came out when guys...no people climaxed. She was fine with that. Hopefully, one day he'd say it and mean it.

She kissed his chest, sighing. The man smelled so freaking terrific, but it was time to move. He didn't like to snuggle. She'd probably already overstayed her welcome. She leaned up and kissed him before moving to her side of the bed.

"What's the matter?" He rolled toward her.

He looked so worried that she smiled. "Nothing. Everything's great."

"Then why are you over there?" He grinned that sexy smile she loved.

"Because you don't like to snuggle."

"I told you before, it's not snuggling with you. It's making sure you're not getting dressed and running for the door."

"I'm not going anywhere. I promise." She touched his cheek. He was so damn handsome but more than that he filled her heart with not just love but hope. "And I don't need to snuggle."

"You really don't mind?"

"No. If you jumped off me as soon as you finished and pushed me away that'd be a problem but holding me all night?" She wrinkled her nose. "Nah. I kind of like my space too."

"Ellie...I..." He kissed her. "I don't know what to say but thanks because I hate snuggling unless it's before sex."

"That's not snuggling, that's foreplay."

"Done right it sure the hell is."

She laughed and slapped his chest. She'd never laughed as much as she did when she was with him. He made everything fun and surprising. "Oh, you know what?"

"No, but you're scaring me."

She grinned at him. "We're together again, right?"

"Don't fuck with me about that. Of course, we're together."

"Then I'm going to open my Valentine's Day gift. I didn't want to unless we were together." She rolled off the bed and headed out of the room.

"Ellie, don't. It's stupid." He sat up. "Come back to bed. I want to snuggle."

"No, you don't," she yelled as she grabbed the present from what she now referred to as the guest room.

"I do. Really," he shouted. "Throw that gift in the trash and we can snuggle every night."

"Now, who's lying." She walked back into the room box in hand.

"I'm not lying." He smirked. "I just didn't say when we'd snuggle."

"I told you. Snuggling before sex is foreplay and it doesn't count as snuggling time." She crawled back onto the bed.

"It counts in my book." He scooted closer to her, kissing her neck. "Seriously, I want to snuggle." His hand squeezed her breast. "Ready for round two in the snuggle fest."

"You're up for that already?" She'd be bowlegged soon if they kept up this pace.

"Not quite, but I'm sure you can think of something to help with that." He ran his finger over her lower lip.

"I can." She twirled her tongue around the tip of his finger.

"That's my girl. Gorgeous and brilliant."

"Gorgeous, brilliant and dying to open her gift. You don't know how it called to me all those nights when I was alone."

"Okay, but you're in for a huge letdown." He propped himself against the headboard. "It's really nothing special."

"I'll love it." She kissed him. "Because you gave it to me." She looked down. "I love the paper." It was red and had little cupids on it. "I'm going to put it with the piece from our Christmas present."

"You still have that?" He seemed surprised.

"Of course." She'd never get rid of that. It reminded

her of when they'd met. She began to unwrap her gift, taking her time as always.

"You don't have to pretend you like it if you don't."

"I won't." She glanced at him. "But I know I'll *love* it." She was being a coward, trying to let him know how she felt without actually saying it.

She gently tore through the last piece of tape and folded the paper, putting it on the nightstand on her side of the bed. She opened the box, moving the tissue aside. It was more wrapping paper. She lifted the top one and then another and another. "It's a box of wrapping paper."

"I told you it was stupid. If you don't like it that's fine. You can give it away or throw it away"

"It's not…" Her throat tightened. Marc had thought she was foolish for saving junk, as he called it. She pulled the stack from the box and placed it on her lap. "Thank you." She was trying hard not to cry as she looked at each package. There were all different colors and styles—some with pictures or patterns, some with glitter and some plain.

"I was going to stop at the jewelry store and get you something else…something better. I didn't actually buy it for you for Valentine's Day," he said.

"You didn't?" She was confused.

"No. I picked a lot of it up weeks ago."

"Weeks ago?" Had he bought it for someone else?

"Yeah. I remembered how much you liked the paper at Christmas so when I went shopping if I saw any that I thought you might like I picked it up. It was a stupid thing to do. I didn't even know you that well. You won't hurt my feelings if you don't want it." He reached over and pulled out one package that was filled with paper in varying shades of pink. "Like this one. I bought it before I knew you didn't like pink." He leaned closer, sliding another one from the stack. "This one, I got after you told me you liked daisies."

"When did you buy this one?" She pointed to the pink one, her hand trembling slightly. She had to be misunderstanding him. If she wasn't, she was going to break down and sob like a baby over the thoughtfulness of his gift. "I don't remember telling you that I don't like pink. I'm okay with pink. I don't hate it."

"You never wear that color, but I didn't know that at the time."

"When? When did you buy it?" She wanted to shake the answer from him.

"Ah, January. A few days after New Year's Eve." His smiled turned wicked. "I looked for stuff with handcuffs, but they don't sell that in Walmart."

"Oh, Adrian." She gave up trying not to cry. There was no holding back the tears. He did care for her. It was the only reason she would've been on his mind for months and not just when he'd been horny.

CHAPTER 44: ADRIAN

"Shit. Don't cry." Adrian hated crying women. He should be used to it with six sisters, but he wasn't. It always ripped out his heart. "I'll buy you something else." Only an idiot would give a woman a box of wrapping paper for Valentine's Day. Roses and chocolates were best sellers for a reason. "I'll throw it away right now. You'll never have to see it again. I promise." He reached for it.

"Don't you dare." Ellie clutched it to her chest.

"But…you hate it. It's making you sad." He was confused. This was one of those times that women didn't make sense at all.

"I don't hate it. I love it."

"Then those are happy tears?" He'd never understand that concept. Ever.

"Yes." She nodded, crying harder. "This is the best gift anyone has ever given to me."

"You really like it?"

She nodded. "I love it." She touched his cheek and kissed him. "Thank you."

"You're welcome." He was happy that she was happy

but more than that she liked his gift. It wasn't much but he'd spent a lot of time choosing these for her. Plus, he'd taken a lot of shit from Mitch about it. "I'm glad you like it." He slid his hand behind her neck and kissed her.

It started gentle but soon he was holding her still while his tongue explored her mouth. He leaned forward, trying to lower her to the mattress. His dick was ready to get back in the game.

She pulled away from him. "Did you mean it?"

"Mean what?" He kissed her neck, not ready to go back to talking.

"I know sometimes guys…Sometimes things are said during sex and they're just words. It's okay."

"Oh. That." He leaned against the headboard again, pretty sure that his dinner was going to come up if they talked about this. He hadn't meant to say it out loud.

"It's okay if you didn't mean it." She kissed him. "But I want you to know that I do mean it."

"What?" He grabbed her shoulder. She couldn't have meant what he thought she'd meant.

"I love you, Adrian." She kissed him again. "I think I have from the moment you flew off the stage to beat up Marc. That's why I fought this so hard. I was terrified." She touched his cheek. "I've never felt like this before and that's why I needed to believe that you were just like Marc and my other exes. I was afraid to admit to myself how wonderful you really are. You're kind, funny, caring, comp…

He grabbed her face. "I love you too, Ellie but I didn't

think you were ready to hear it." He kissed her and it was slow and hot and filled with love. "Don't ever be afraid with me. I'll never hurt you. As a matter of fact, I'll kick anyone's ass who even tries to hurt you." His eyes narrowed. "And you'd better not think, even for one second, that I can't. Got it?"

"Got it." She smiled, running her fingers through his hair.

"Now, you need to finish your list of all the great things I am." He kissed her again.

"I do?"

"Yeah." He lowered her to the bed. "You owe me. You've been rough on my ego."

"Ha. Your ego is stronger than steel."

"A part of me is harder than steel." He shifted, pressing his cock against her thigh. "Let me help you get started. Adrian is sexy, a fabulous lover, brilliant..."

"Brilliant?"

"Yep." He kissed her neck.

"I think I should take over from here."

"Be my guest." He kissed his way down her chest.

"Adrian is...arrogant, conceited..."

"I don't think you understand the concept of stroking a man's ego." He licked her nipple, loving how her fingers tugged his hair.

"Trust me. I know how to stroke...your ego."

He grinned up at her. "I think you'll need to prove that." He gently bit down on her nipple, making her writhe beneath him.

"Let…me…finish." She was breathless. "He eats like a child"—her hand covered his mouth before he could protest—"and he's cocky." She reached between his legs, wrapping her hand around his growing dick. "Considerate." She pushed on his chest, rolling him to his back. "Loyal." Her lips trailed across his abdomen. "And one kickass fighter." Her mouth closed around the tip of his cock.

"Fuck, Ellie." His hips arched upward, pushing his dick farther into her mouth. He leaned on his elbows, watching as she bobbed up and down, his dick disappearing inside her mouth. "Fuck, I love you."

She pulled off him. "I love you too." She smiled, wide and happy and his balls tightened.

"Ellie, I'm close."

"Good, because another one of your wonderful qualities is that you taste fantastic." She lowered her mouth to his cock, pulling him deep inside.

"Fuck." He should stop her, but it felt too damn good. "I'll take care of you next. I swear."

She lifted off him again, a smile in her eyes. "I trust you."

He nodded, lost for words because he could see in her eyes that she wasn't lying. She licked his tip and then sucked his cock. He dropped back onto the mattress, lost in his two favorite things, happiness and pleasure.

Thanks for reading the Cupid's Misfire (book 3 in the Hot Holiday series). I hope you enjoyed Adrian and Ellie's story.

Want to read about how Ethan and La Petite Mort Club helped to save Liz and Craig's marriage?

Or maybe you want to meet more of the gorgeous and kinky men and women of La Petite Mort Club.

Just check out the excerpts. There's one for the following books:

A Merry Masquerade for Christmas. Craig and Liz are headed for a divorce over a misunderstanding. Can one night of kinky fun at a masquerade ball save their marriage?

His Sub (free ebook) — Terry's a dominant but Maggie's not his usual sub. She's a curvy, single mother of three who needs a dominant's guidance more than any woman he's ever met. However, she insists on fighting him every step of the way.

Interviewing for her Lover (free ebook) — Nick's the consummate playboy. Sarah is looking for a lover for a few nights. They should be perfect for each other and they are. Too perfect. Their chemistry is off-the-charts explosive. Will they be able to walk away after only six nights of fantasies? (this book is the first of their six nights together).

The Voyeur (free ebook)–See how Patrick (Adrian's boss) and Annie meet. She's a maid who likes to watch people having sex at the Club. He's given the job of keeping her out of trouble, but he's the biggest danger to her because no matter how hard he tries, he just can't keep his hands off her.

Plus, if you sign up for my newsletter, you can get the entire Six Nights of Sin series for free (all six nights of Nick and Sarah's contract—every delicious fantasy) as a thank you gift.

Go to my website to join and get your free book.

Here's What You Get When You
Join My Readers' Group

Win Before You Can Buy
Exclusive Giveaways
Free Books
Sneak Peeks

Go to my website or email me for details:

www.EllisODay.com

authorEllisOday@gmail.com

Liz shoved the mop across the floor. She always cleaned when she was upset. Her house was going to be spotless. This was all so unfair and so typical. Craig was going to a party—a masked party on Christmas Eve. She'd be sitting home, crying and watching *It's a Wonderful Life,* while her husband would be having the time of his life with some other woman. She snorted. Nothing new there. He'd been doing it for years.

Her phone beeped. That'd better not be him needing something else. She'd skewer him with the mop handle if she had to see him again.

She put the mop down and walked into the kitchen to grab her phone. Damn, he'd looked good yesterday—his body strong and lean, his dark brown hair a little too long. When she'd turned and he'd been looking at her with desire…no hot lust, she'd almost fallen into his arms. She hated that she still wanted him. He'd never change. He'd always cheat—her father had, her sister's husband had. Craig wouldn't be any different, especially with a membership to that club.

She grabbed her phone off the counter and stared at her messages. This had to be a mistake, but it wasn't. It was a blessing.

Come and check out The Christmas Eve Bash. Mask Required. Clothing Optional. Doors open at 6 pm. Non-members show this message for entry.

This had to be the party Craig was attending. Ethan must've forgotten to remove her from the potential client list. It was her own Christmas miracle. She hurried to the garage. She had to find a mask. She was going to show Craig that she wasn't just his wife—soon to be ex-wife. She was a woman who needed a man and she was still attractive enough to get one.

Find out what happens next.

https://ellisoday.com/books/a-merry-masquerade-for-

Ellis O. Day

christmas/

Free - His Sub

Terry wandered through the crowd of well-dressed women and men at La Petite Mort Club. It was the same scene every time Ethan, his friend and owner of the Club, threw one of these events. The members mingled with the newbies, hoping to snag something different or someone interesting.

Ethan strolled casually toward him, a ready smile on his face as he greeted his guests. "Terry, about time you made it down here."

"Like you can talk." His friend spent most of his time

in the back office, watching the Club on monitors.

"I've been mingling for over an hour."

"It's your business not mine." He leaned against the balustrade, peering down on the crowd.

"True, but you could sell your practice and buy me out."

"And run this place?" He laughed. "No thank you." He tossed back his scotch. "I spend enough time here as it is." He used to practically live here except when he was at the office or in court, but lately he'd been staying home more.

"Good turn out tonight." Ethan waved at a waitress and a moment later they each had another drink.

"Yeah, but I don't see one interesting person in this crop of wannabe members."

"And you can tell if someone is interesting just by looking at them?"

"I can tell not one of them has an original thought. Look at them. They're all in red." The Club was awash in a sea of red dresses—short, long, dark, light but always red.

"It is a Valentine's Day party."

"I know but you'd think one woman"—he held up his finger—"one would consider that everyone else would be in red and wear a different color."

"There are some pinks out there."

"Same thing, just lighter."

Ethan grabbed his phone from his pocket and looked at the text, frowning.

"Problem?" The Club was usually a safe place but on open night events, when Ethan allowed non-members access in order to recruit new members, the place could get dangerous.

"A little skirmish over a woman." Ethan grinned, his blue eyes sparkling as a couple of young guys hurried past them, almost tripping in their haste to stay close to a group of very attractive women. "These youngsters haven't learned that sharing is more fun."

He ignored Ethan's teasing. He'd taken a lot of shit from Ethan, Nick and even Patrick because he wasn't into the sharing thing. He preferred it to be him and one woman, one sweet, little sub. Since he was in no mood to listen to any more crap, he'd change the subject. "Those kids barely look old enough to drink."

"You're showing your age." Ethan patted his shoulder. "You should find some nice, young thing and teach her how to please her master."

"Maybe I will, if any of them show enough originality to dress in something other than red."

"I've got to go and sort out this problem." Ethan slid his phone into his pocket. "I'll find you later. If you find that elusive non-red dress, I'd suggest we share but..." He chuckled as he headed down the stairs, maneuvering through the crowd like he had nowhere to go, when in reality he was heading for the back—the playrooms.

Terry's eyes stopped and lingered on the new hire, Desiree, who was moving around the room, talking and flirting with all the men and some women. She was interesting—exotic and smart—but there was a shrewdness behind her eyes that he'd learned a long time ago to avoid.

A woman like her had an agenda and she stuck with it, no matter what.

Someone slammed into his back, causing his drink to spill down his front, staining his shirt and suit.

"Oh…oh, I'm so sorry."

He spun around and encountered a red dress and breasts—milky white and lush. The skin would be fragrant and softer than rose petals.

"Oh. Your shirt. Let me get something to wipe that up."

He forced his eyes away from those lovely breasts. Her hair was a rich mahogany. It'd probably hang past her shoulders in waves of curly silk but right now it was piled haphazardly on her head in what had been some kind of elegant style before disobedient strands had escaped their restraint. She looked mussed and damnit, he wanted to be the one to muss her.

"Paper towels? Napkins?" She glanced around and then hurried over to the bar.

She was short and curvy—her body succulent, ripe and he'd bet juicy. She grabbed a stack of napkins and headed for him. Her dress was too tight, like she'd recently gained some weight. He usually went for the tall, athletic types but for some reason his dick had picked this woman.

She returned to his side and dabbed at the wetness on his shirt and jacket as if she actually gave a shit about his clothes. This was no subtle caress, no flirtation—just indifferent efficiency.

"I'm so sorry." She wadded the napkins in her hand,

162

still patting at his clothes.

"You said that already." His words came out gruffer than he'd meant. No one treated him with disinterest. He was a rich, successful, attractive man and she was treating him like a child. He wanted to pull up her—unfortunately, red—dress and fuck her right here. They were at the Club. It wasn't out of the question.

Her hand froze. "Oh." Her large hazel eyes looked startled and then hurt. "Sorry. Ah, excuse me." She headed toward the stairs, dropping the wet napkins in the trash before disappearing in the crowd.

He turned around, so he could see the first floor and waited for her to appear. She hurried across the downstairs room, bumping and stumbling through the crowd. A lone, scared, little rabbit in a room full of predators. She stopped for a moment, scanning the crowd as if searching for someone.

"Who are you looking for, little rabbit?" he mumbled to himself. "A husband? Boyfriend?" He grinned as he lifted his scotch to his lips. "Girlfriend?" He frowned at the empty glass. "You spilled my drink. I'll forgive you, but it's going to cost you." He waved at one of the waitresses. "Everything has a price, little rabbit." As one of the best divorce lawyers in town, he knew that better than anyone.

The waitress brought him another drink. He paid, giving her a large tip before turning to find his little rabbit. He took a sip of the scotch, enjoying the smooth burn and his lush little bunny's journey through La Petite Mort Club. She froze in her tracks, her jaw dropping open as she gazed at a threesome on one of the couches.

The woman was sandwiched between two men, stroking one's cock as the other man fondled her beneath her red dress. The man behind her looked up and said something to the little rabbit. Her face heated and Terry's eyes dropped to her chest. Yep, they were a pretty shade of pink but what he really wanted to know was if the color matched her pussy.

She stumbled away from the threesome, bumping into another man. It was Richard, who stopped her from falling and then immediately let her go, stepping away. She was safe with Richard. As a member of the Club and a gentleman, he knew that safewords were law and consent was absolutely necessary. She said something to Richard and continued through the Club, disappearing in the crowd.

"You're not getting away that easily." He followed along on the upper floor, keeping her in sight. He had no idea why but he wanted her. Maybe it was simply because she was different than everyone else here.

He took another sip of his drink. It was obviously the little rabbit's first time at a place like this but she didn't seem eager to participate or interested in watching. She truly seemed to be looking for someone specific—not just someone to fuck. Well, she'd found the latter because he was going to fuck her. In the office he followed his head but at La Petite Mort Club his cock was king.

She headed toward the playrooms. There was no way he was going to miss this. He sauntered down the stairs, grabbing another drink on the way. She wasn't hard to follow. She left a path of irritated people in her wake as she bumped into them and apologized profusely before hurrying forward. Her full, round hips swayed under her tight, red dress that'd seen better days—hem frayed and at least five years out of style. Not that he minded, especially the snug fit of the cloth, but his women were usually much more put tougher.

They were the CEO types—women who thrived on being in charge. He enjoyed teaching them how much fun turning over control could be. When they were with him, he was their dom, their master and he made sure they loved every second. He told them when to kneel, when to suck, when to spread their legs or ass and when to come. The more power they had in their everyday life the more they craved bowing to his wishes. His little rabbit wouldn't know what power was. She was a hot mess of a woman. Still, his dick wanted her, so his dick would have her.

She was hurrying out of the first playroom when he entered the hallway. Her eyes were huge and her cheeks were on fire. She ducked into the next room and quickly came out—even redder than before.

"Excuse me." He'd offer his assistance in her search. She'd be grateful. He could capitalize on that unless she was looking for her husband or boyfriend. He wasn't in the mood to share. He would, however, allow the other man to watch. He could give the guy some pointers on how to take care of his wife because this woman obviously needed guidance.

"You?" Her eyes narrowed.

That wasn't the reaction he was used to. Women usually purred for him.

"Are you following me?"

"What would you do if I said I was?" He took a step toward her.

"I'd scream. There are bouncers here. I saw them."

Lord, she was cute. "Yes, but if they came running at every little scream they'd die of exhaustion."

As if to emphasis his point a woman screamed in ecstasy. His little rabbit's face heated and she averted her gaze.

"Who are you looking for?" He ran his finger lightly down her cheek. Her skin was as smooth as porcelain but much warmer and softer.

"Ah…" Her breath hitched, making her breasts swell dangerously above her gown.

He could have her out of it in a minute. The skin would be even softer than that on her face. "Did you lose your husband?"

"No." She licked her lips.

There was no way he could let that offer pass. He slowly bent, giving her time to refuse him. He may command his women but he made sure they always wanted it first. Her eyes dropped to his mouth and he couldn't help a slight smirk. She wanted this as much as he did. He moved closer and let his lips rest gently on hers. He'd take it slow, make her yearn for him and then he'd make her obey.

"What are you doing?" She turned her head.

166

"Kissing you." His lips brushed against her cheek. He wasn't about to lose ground.

"Why?" She turned again, her eyes meeting his.

The confusion in her hazel gaze was as obvious as the hideous dress on her gorgeous body. She may remind him of a rabbit but she couldn't be that naive. She had to be in her mid to late thirties.

He should use flowery words—tell her she was beautiful, desirable—but that wasn't him. Blunt was the kindest word to describe him. "Because, I want to."

"You don't even know me."

He was losing ground. The interest in her face was being replaced with disgust. "No, but I know I want you." Damn, he shouldn't have said that.

"Well, too bad." She pushed on his chest and he stepped back, letting her pass.

"This is a sex club, you know." He followed. "If you aren't here for sex, why are you here?"

She spun around. "I'm quite aware of what this place is and just because I don't want you, a stranger to…to"—she waved her hand about—"in the hallway."

He laughed. "We wouldn't be the first. There are people fucking in the main room."

"I know. I saw." Her cheeks heated.

He stepped closer. "You are adorable." He touched a strand of hair that was resting on her shoulder. It was like satin.

"I'm a mess." She pulled her hair free from his fingers.

"A hot mess. A fiery, hot, sexy mess." He moved

closer with every other word. "One I want to fuck, right now."

Her eyes hardened. "Too bad because I don't"—again she waved her hand about—"you know, with strangers in the hallway." She shoved his chest again.

He took a small step back but he wasn't giving up yet. "We can go to a private room."

"No."

Shit. By the look on her face, he'd just made a bigger blunder.

"Let me go." She pushed him again.

Damn. She'd said the worst three words in the English language besides I love you. He moved away, releasing her for the moment. "Sorry."

She harrumphed.

"I made a mistake."

"Yes, you did." She hurried down the hallway but not before he'd seen the look of hurt in her large eyes.

"What the fuck do you want from me? I made a mistake and apologized." He trailed after her.

"I want you to leave me alone. Please. Go away."

He stopped. His little rabbit was running but perhaps, he shouldn't chase. She darted down a hallway toward the hardcore BDSM rooms.

Normally, she'd be fine—embarrassed but fine. Except with all the newbies here, tonight wasn't a normal night. He hurried after her. "Hey, I don't think you want to go—"

"Leave me alone." She walked faster. "I need to find my friend and get out of here."

"Okay, but I don't—"

"Go away." She sounded both mad and as if she were going to cry.

"Suit yourself, but I warned you."

She strode into the closest room. He should leave. Let her find out that he wasn't the worst thing in a place like this, not in a long shot, but his feet followed her. She was his little rabbit. He'd found her. No one else was going to enjoy her until he'd had his taste.

"Vicky? Vicky? Are you in here?"

He stepped into the room, staying in the shadows. She was looking around in the dark for her friend. It only took a moment for one of the six guys to notice the little rabbit who'd stumbled into their den.

"Shit," he mumbled. Not one of those guys was a regular.

Grab your free copy and find out what happens next.
You can find the book on my website
https://ellisoday.com/books/free-his-sub/

Free: Interviewing For Her Lover

"Do I have to take off my clothes?" Sarah tugged on the hem of her black dress. It was shorter and lower cut in the front than she normally wore, but the Viewing was about finding a man for sex and according to Ethan men liked to look.

"No." Ethan turned her away from the door and forced her to look at him. "You don't have to do anything you don't want to do."

She stared into his blue eyes. Why couldn't he be interested in her? She'd only met with him five or six times, but she trusted him. He ran his business, La Petite

Mort Club, very professionally and he was gorgeous with his sandy brown hair, strong cheekbones and vibrant blue eyes. Sex between them would be good. Easy. He was attractive and...not for her. She didn't want decent sex or good sex, she wanted mind blowing, screaming orgasms and that wouldn't happen between him and her because there was no chemistry, no attraction.

"Listen to me." He moved his hands to her shoulders and gave her a gentle shake. "You aren't selling yourself to the highest bidder. You're looking for a partner. One who'll"—he grinned—"turn you on in ways you can't even imagine."

She glanced at the door where the men waited. Waited for her. Waited to decide if they wanted to fuck her. "I'm a bit nervous."

"About what?"

This was embarrassing, but she'd been honest with him up to this point. She'd had to be. He was helping her...had helped her to choose the five men in the other room. "What if none of them..."

"They will want you." He touched her chin, turning her face toward him. "A few of them may back out after this but not because they don't want you."

"Yeah, right."

"I'm only going to say this once. You're beautiful and different, unique."

"That's not necessarily a good thing." She had long legs and a nice body—trim and firm—but with her auburn hair and green eyes she was cute at best, not gorgeous. The men she'd chosen were all rich, good looking and powerful. They could have anyone they wanted.

"It's exactly what they want, or most of them anyway." He took her hand and led her closer to the door.

She leaned on his arm, hating these shoes. She should've stuck with her flats but Ethan had given her a list of what she should wear and high heels were on the top. She'd found the smallest heels in the store and by Ethan's look when he'd first seen her she might've been better off going barefoot. He'd met her at the private entrance and his gaze had been appreciating as it'd skimmed over her dress until he got to her feet. Then he'd frowned and shook his head.

"Finding the right men for you wasn't easy." He stopped at the door.

"Thanks a lot." She shifted away from him, his words hurting a little. She hadn't been sure of her appeal to the opposite sex in a long time, not since the early years with Adam.

"It's not because you aren't beautiful but because you want to be dominated and you want to dominate—"

"I do not want to dominate." All she could picture was a woman in black leather with a whip and that wasn't her, not at all.

"If you say so." He smiled a little. "But, you do want to lead the scene. Right? Because that's what—"

"Yes." Her face was red. She could feel it. She didn't want to talk about her fantasies again. It'd been embarrassing enough the first time, but he'd had to know what she wanted to compile a list of candidates.

"Most at the club are either doms or subs. Very few are switches." His eyes raked over her. "That's what's so special about you. You want it all and…that's what made choosing these men difficult."

He'd given her a selection of twenty-two men who might be interested in what she wanted. She'd narrowed it down to seven. Two had been uninterested when he'd approached. That'd left her with the five who'd see her in person for the first time tonight, but she wouldn't see them. That'd come after the Viewing when she interviewed any who were still interested.

"Remember what you want. This is your deal. You call the shots. At least a little." He kissed her forehead. "But don't refuse to give them anything. You don't want a submissive."

"No." That didn't turn her on at all and she only had eight weeks. One night each week for two months before she'd go back to her lonely life, her lonely bed, dreaming of Adam.

"You can do this." He pulled a flask from his jacket and unscrewed the lid. "For courage."

"Thanks." She took a large swallow, the brandy too thick and sweet for her taste but it was better than nothing.

"Now, go find your lover."

She laughed a little but sadness swept through her. There'd be no love between this man and herself. This would be sex, fucking. That's all. The only man she'd ever love, her only lover, was dead. This was purely physical. "Thank you again." She stood on tip-toe and kissed his cheek. He may be gorgeous and run a sex club but he was a good man, a good friend.

She turned and opened the door and walked into the room, trying to stay balanced on these stupid heels. Men wouldn't find them so attractive if they had to wear them. The room was dark except for one light highlighting a small platform. That was for her. She stepped up onto the small stage. The room was silent but they were there, above her, hidden behind the one-way mirrors, watching and deciding if they wanted to take the next step—to eventually take her.

She stared into the blackness of the room. It wasn't huge but its emptiness made it seem vast. She glanced upward, the light making her squint and she quickly stared back into the darkness. This was arranged for them to see her. That was it. She'd get no glimpse of them yet. She'd seen their pictures, chosen them but meeting them in person would be different. A picture couldn't tell her their smell or the sound of their voices.

She tugged at her dress where it hugged her hips, wishing the questions would start, but there was only silence. She shifted, the heels already killing her feet. Ethan hadn't liked them and if they weren't going to impress, she might as well take them off. She moved to the back of the stage, leaned against the wall and removed her shoes. As she returned to the center of the stage a man spoke, his voice loud and commanding almost echoing throughout the room.

"Don't stop there. Take off your dress."

She bent, placing her shoes on the floor. That wasn't part of the deal. She wasn't going to undress in front of five men, only one. Only the one she chose. She straightened. "No."

"What?" He was surprised and not happy.

"I said no. That's not part of the Viewing."

"I want to see what I'm getting."

She stared up toward the windows, squinting a little. She couldn't tell from where the voice had come. The speaker system made it sound as if it were coming from God himself. "And you will if I pick you."

Another man laughed.

"It's not funny. She's disobedient," said the man with the loud voice.

"Not always. I can be obedient." These men liked to be in control but sometimes, so did she.

"Will you raise your dress? Just a little," asked another voice.

"Didn't you see enough in the photos?" She'd applied a few months ago for this one-time contract. She'd been excited and nervous when she'd received the acceptance email with an appointment for a photography session. She'd never had her picture professionally taken, since she didn't count school portraits or the ones her parents had had done at JCPenny's. She'd been anxious and a little turned on imaging wearing her new lingerie in front of a strange man, so she'd been disappointed to find the photographer was an elderly woman, but the lady had put her at ease and

175

the photos had turned out better than she'd expected. She glanced up at the mirrors, hoping she wasn't disappointing all the men. That'd be too embarrassing.

"Those were…nice, but I'd like to see the real thing before deciding if you're worth my time."

She raised a brow. "You can always leave." She shouldn't antagonize him. She was sure the bossy man had already decided against committing to this agreement. Disobedience didn't appeal to him. That left four. If she didn't pick any of them, she could go through the process again, but she didn't think she would.

The man chuckled slightly. "I know that, but I haven't decided I don't want to fuck you. Not yet, anyway."

The word, so harsh and vulgar excited her. It was the truth. That was what she, what they were all deciding. Who'd get to fuck her. It was what she wanted, what she'd agreed to do, and as much as she dreaded it, she wanted it. She was tired of being alone. She missed having a man inside her—his tongue and fingers and cock.

"Do any of you have any questions?" She clasped her dress at her waist and slowly gathered it upward, displaying more and more of her long legs. She ran. They were in shape. The men would like them.

"Lower your top," said the same man who'd told her to take off her dress.

She didn't like him. If he didn't back out, she'd have Ethan remove him from her list. He was too commanding. He'd never allow her to be in control.

"I don't know if he's done looking at my legs yet."

She continued raising the dress until her black and green lace panties were almost exposed.

"Very nice and thank you," said the polite man.

"You're welcome." This man might work. She shifted the dress up another inch before dropping it, giving them a glance at her panties.

"Now, your top," said the bossy guy.

She lowered her spaghetti string off one shoulder, letting the dress dip, but not enough to show anything besides the side of her bra.

"More," he said.

"No." She raised the strap, covering herself. She didn't like this man and wished he'd leave. She'd kick him out but that wasn't part of the process and they were very firm about their rules at this club.

"He got to see your pussy. Why don't I get to see your tits?"

"You got to see as much as he did." She was ready to move on. She bent and picked up her shoes. "If there's nothing else, gentleman, we can set up times for the interview process."

"Turn around," said another man.

It was a command, but she didn't mind. There was a politeness to his order and something about the texture of his voice caused an ache between her thighs. There was a caress in his tone but with an edge and a promise of a good hard fuck.

"Are you going to obey?" His words were whisper soft and smooth.

"Yes." That was going to be part of this too. Her commanding and him commanding. She dropped her shoes and turned.

"Raise you dress again."

She looked over her shoulder at where she imagined he sat watching her.

"Please." There was humor in his tone.

She smiled and slowly gathered the dress upward. She stopped right below the curve of her bottom.

"More. Please." There was a little less humor in his voice.

She wanted to show him her ass. She wanted to show that voice everything but not with the others around. This would be just her and one man, one stranger. That was one of her rules. "No. Only if you're picked do you get to see any more of me than you have." She dropped her dress, grabbed her shoes and walked off the stage and out the door.

She was going to have sex with a stranger. She was going to live out her fantasies for eight nights with a man she didn't know and would never really know, but she wasn't going to lose who she was. She'd keep her honor and her dignity which meant she had to pick a man who'd agree with her rules.

Get your free copy and find out what happens next.

https://books2read.com/u/3nYKo6

Free: The Voyeur

Annie finished making the bed and gathered the sheets from the floor, keeping them as far away from her body as possible. These sex rooms were disgusting and Ethan was a jerk making her work as a maid. She almost had her Bachelor's Degree in Culinary Arts, but he'd refused to hire her for the kitchen—too many men in the kitchen. The only job he'd give her at La Petite Mort Club was as a maid and unfortunately, she needed the money too badly to refuse.

She stuffed the dirty sheets into the cart and hurried out the door. She had almost thirty minutes before she had to be at the next "sex room." She hid the cart in a closet and darted down a back hallway, staying clear of the cameras. Julie, the woman who supervised the daytime maids, was a real bitch. If she were caught sneaking away from her duties, she'd be assigned to the orgy rooms every day. Right now, they all took turns cleaning that nightmare. She swore they should get hazard pay to even go in those rooms.

She slipped through a doorway and hurried to the one-way mirror. She stared at the couple in the next room. From her first day here, she'd been curious about the activities at the club. She was twenty-four and wasn't a virgin but she'd never, ever done some of these things.

The woman in the room below was tied to a table, legs spread and wearing some sort of leather outfit that left her large breasts free and her crotch exposed. She had shaved her pussy and her pink lower lips were swollen and glistening from her excitement. The man strolled around the table as if he had all night. He still had his pants on but had removed his shirt. His arms and chest were well defined but he had a slight paunch. His erection tented his pants and Annie felt wetness pool between her legs. She had no idea why watching this turned her on but it did. Ever since she'd accidentally barged in on that guy and girl in the Interview room, she couldn't stop watching.

The man below ran his hand up the woman's inner thigh, glancing over her pussy. The woman thrust her hips upward and Annie ran her own hand between her legs. The man's mouth moved but Annie couldn't hear anything and then he slapped the woman across the thigh hard enough to leave a red mark. Annie jumped. She wasn't into that, but she couldn't stop watching the woman's face. At first, it'd contorted in pain but then it'd morphed into pleasure. The man hit her again and then bent, kissing the red welts— running his tongue across them as his fingers squeezed her nipple.

Annie clutched her thighs together, searching for some relief. Her panties were soaked. It wouldn't take but a few strokes to make her come. She started to slide her hand into her pants.

"Having fun?" asked a deep voice from behind her.

She spun around, her heart dropping into her stomach. "Ah…I was just finishing cleaning in here." Damn, she should've closed the door but she hadn't expected anyone in this area. The rooms were off limits on this floor until tonight and she was the only one assigned to clean here.

He shut the door and locked it before strolling toward her. She'd seen him around the Club, but more than that she remembered him from the military photos her brother, Vic, had sent to her. She carried one of the three of them—Vic, Ethan and this guy, Patrick—in her purse. He'd been attractive in the picture, but now that he was older and in person he was gorgeous. He had dark green eyes, brown hair and a perfect body. He stopped so close to her his chest almost brushed against her breasts. She was pretty sure it would if she inhaled deeply. She really wanted to take that deep breath and feel his hard chest against her breasts.

"Don't let me stop you from enjoying the show."

"I…I wasn't. I should go." She started to walk past him but he grabbed her hand.

His grip was warm and strong but loose enough that she could pull free if she wanted. She didn't. Even though she only knew him from her brother's pictures and letters, she'd had many fantasies about him when she'd been in high school. Her gaze dropped to the front of his pants and her mouth almost watered. He was definitely interested. She dragged her eyes up his body, stopping on his face. He smiled at her.

"There's nothing to be embarrassed about. Watching turns us all on." He kissed the back of her hand and she jumped as his tongue darted out, tasting her skin.

"I…I should go." She didn't move.

"No, you should watch." He dropped her hand and grabbed her shoulders, gently turning her toward the mirror. He trailed his hands up and down her arms. "Watch."

The man in the other room was now sucking on the woman's breast as his fingers caressed her pussy.

"Would you like to hear them? Or do you like it quiet?" His voice was a rough whisper against her ear.

"Sound, please." She wanted to hear their gasps and moans. She wanted to close her eyes and pretend it was her. She shifted, squeezing her thighs together.

He chuckled as he moved away. She felt his absence to her bones. He'd been strong and warm behind her and for a moment she'd felt safe, safer than she had since her brother had come back from the war, broken and sad, and her father had started drinking again.

The woman's moans filled the room and Patrick came back to stand behind her, this time placing his hands on her waist.

"I'm Patrick," he said against her ear.

She couldn't take her eyes from the scene in front of her. The woman was almost coming as the man thrust his fingers inside of her.

"What's your name?" He nipped her neck and she jumped.

"I...I..." If she told him her name, he might say something to Ethan. Ethan would kill her if he knew she was in here watching.

"Tell me your name." His lips trailed along her neck and she tipped her head giving him better access.

The guy was kissing his way down the woman's body. Annie wanted to touch herself, to make herself come but Patrick was here.

He nibbled her ear. "Why won't you tell me your name?"

"I...I'll get in trouble." She rubbed her ass against his erection, hopefully giving him a hint.

"Tease." His hand drifted down her stomach, stopping right above where she wanted him to touch. "Tell me your name or I'll make you suffer." He unbuttoned her pants and left his hand—warm, rough but immobile—resting on her abdomen.

"I can't." She stood on tip-toe, hoping his hand would lower a little but he was too tall or she was too short. He had to be almost six foot and she was barely five-foot four. "I could get fired and I need this job."

"Darling, Ethan won't fire you for fucking a customer."

"We can't." She spun around. She hadn't thought this through. He was her fantasy come to life and she wanted him to be hers just for a moment, but Ethan would find out and then she'd be in deep shit.

"Don't worry. I'm a member and you work here, so we're both clean." He hesitated, his hands tightening on her hips. "Are you protected?"

"What?" She had no idea what he was talking about.

"Ethan makes sure everyone at the Club is clean but only the…some of his employees are required to be on birth control." He ran his hands up her sides, getting closer and closer to her breasts. "Are you on birth control?" His eyes darkened as they dropped to her tits. "If not, it's okay. There are other things we can do."

Oh, she wanted to do everything his eyes promised, but she couldn't. "No, I'll get in trouble. I need this job. I have to go." She tried to move but her feet refused to obey, so she just stared at his handsome face.

"Are you sure?" He bent so he was almost eye level with her. "I promise. Ethan won't care. A lot of maids become…change jobs. The pay's a lot better." His eyes roamed over her frame. "Especially, for someone as cute as you."

Ethan would kill her before letting her become one of his pleasure associates.

"I could talk to Ethan for you." His hands moved up her body, stopping right below her breasts.

Her nipples hardened and she forgot everything but what he was making her feel. He ran his thumb over one of them and she leaned closer, wanting him to do it again.

He did. He continued rubbing her nipple as he spoke. "I could persuade him to let me…handle your initiation into club life."

Her heart raced in her chest. It could be just her and him doing all these things she'd seen. Her pussy throbbed but she couldn't do it. She wouldn't do it. She couldn't have sex for money. Her parents were both dead but they'd never understand and she couldn't disappoint them. "No. I can't do that…not for money." Her eyes darted to the door. She needed to get out of there before she did something she'd regret.

"That's even better." He smiled as he stepped closer. "We can keep this between us. No money. Only a man and a woman." He leaned down and whispered in her ear, "Giving each other pleasure. A lot of pleasure. In ways you haven't even imagined."

There were moans from the other room and she glanced over her shoulder. The man's face was buried between the woman's thighs.

Patrick turned her around, pulling her against him and wrapping his arms around her waist. "Are you wet?"

"What? No." She struggled in his arms, her ass brushing against his erection again.

"Oh fuck. Do that again." He kissed her neck, open mouthed and hot.

She stopped trying to get away. She wanted this...this moment. She shouldn't but she did, so she wiggled her butt against him again. He was hard and long and her body ached for him. It'd been too long she'd had sex. She needed this.

"Would you like me to touch you?" His hands drifted over her hips and down her thighs.

She'd like him to do all sorts of things to her. She nodded.

"Say it." His words were a command she couldn't disobey.

"Yes."

"Yes, what?" He untucked her shirt from her pants.

"Touch me. Please." She was already pushing her hips toward his hand. She wanted his hand on her, his fingers inside of her.

"Are you wet?" he asked again.

She inhaled sharply as he unzipped her pants.

"Don't lie to me. I'll find out in a minute."

She'd never talked dirty during sex and she wasn't sure she was ready to do that with a stranger. Her heart skipped a beat. Maybe, she shouldn't be doing any of this with a stranger. She grabbed his hand. "Maybe, we shouldn't."

The woman below cried out and the man straightened, wiping his face and unbuttoning his pants.

"Watch. The main event is about to happen." Patrick's hot breath tickled her neck.

Her gaze locked on the man's penis. It was large and demanding. He straddled the woman, grabbing his cock.

"Don't you want to feel some of what they feel?" He nibbled on her ear and then neck. "I can help you."

She may not know him, but she trusted him. He was a former marine. He'd been a good friend of Vic's. He wouldn't hurt her and she needed to come. She loosened her grip, letting go of his hand. He slipped inside her pants, caressing her pussy through her underwear. His fingers were long and strong. She closed her eyes, leaning against him as he stroked her.

"You're already so wet and hot." His breath was a warm caress on her ear. "But, I'm going to make you wetter and then, I'm going to make you come." His other hand shoved her pants down, giving him more room to work. "Open your eyes and watch the show."

She did as he said. The man was inside the woman, thrusting hard and fast. The woman was moaning and trying to move but the restraints kept her mostly helpless.

"Fuck, you're soaked." Patrick's hand cupped her and she arched into his touch, rubbing her ass against his erection. He shoved his hand inside her underwear, his finger running along her folds until he slipped one inside.

"Oh." She grabbed his hand—not to push him away, but to make sure he didn't leave.

He smiled against her hair. "Don't worry, baby. I won't stop." He stroked his finger inside of her and his wrist brushed against her clit.

She needed more. She needed to touch him, feel him. She turned her head, wrapping her arms up and around his neck. He kissed her. It was desperate and wild, but he stopped too soon.

"They're almost done. You don't want to miss it."

She turned back to the mirror. The man below continued to fuck the woman as Patrick finger-fucked her. His other hand slipped under her shirt to her breast. His lips sucked her neck as he rocked his erection against her ass. He was everywhere, and she was so close. The muscles in her legs constricted. Her hips tipped upward.

"Wait, baby," he groaned in her ear, as he pushed a second finger inside of her. "Just a few more minutes."

His fingers were stretching her and it felt wonderful. She moaned, long and low as he thrust harder and faster, almost matching the pace of the man in the other room. She could almost imagine it was Patrick's cock and not his fingers inside of her.

"Oh…oh," she cried out. He was pushing her toward the edge. Her body was spiraling with each pump of his fingers. She was going to come—right here while watching that couple. It was so dirty and so wrong and it only made her hotter.

The woman below screamed and her body stiffened. The man thrust again and again and then grunted his release.

"Show's over." Patrick nipped her neck at the same time he pressed down on her clit with his thumb, sending her shooting into her orgasm.

She trembled and he pulled her close, his hand still cupping her pussy and his fingers still inside of her. When her heartbeat had settled, he removed his hand and bent, pulling off her shoes and removing her pants before lifting her and carrying her to the wall.

"My turn." He wrapped her legs around his waist.

Her phone rang. "My work phone. I...I have to answer it."

"When we're done." He unzipped his pants.

"Annie, answer the phone. I know you're around here. I can hear it ringing you stupid bitch," yelled Julie.

"Oh, shit." She shoved Patrick away, and ran across the room, grabbing her clothes off the floor. "It's my boss. She'll kill me if she finds me like this."

"I'll take care of Julie." He headed for the door, zipping up his fly. "Don't move." He grinned over his shoulder at her. "You can take off your pants again, but other than that, don't move."

"No. Please." She raced over to him, grabbing his arm. "I need this job." And Ethan could not find out about this.

"She won't fire you. She can't. Only Ethan can fire you." He bent and kissed her.

His lips were gentle and coaxing this time and her body swayed into him. He pulled her even closer and she could feel his cock, thick and heavy, pushing against her. Her pussy tightened again in anticipation.

"Damn it, Annie. This is going to be so much worse if I have to call your stupid phone again. Get out here!" Julie was only a few doors down.

She grabbed Patrick and tugged on his hand. "Please, hide." She glanced around, looking for somewhere that would conceal a six-foot muscular man.

"I'm not going to hide from Julie."

Get Your FREE Copy and find out what happens next.

HTTPS://BOOKS2READ.COM/U/BXQBMK

BOOKS BY ELLIS O. DAY
OR SEE THEM ALL ON MY WEBSITE
HTTPS://WWW.ELLISODAY.COM

LA PETITE MORT CLUB SERIES

THE BILLIONAIRE'S BABY
https://ellisoday.com/books/the-billionaires-baby
The Baby Bargain (book 1) (free)
https://books2read.com/thebabybargain
Making the Baby (book 2)
https://ellisoday.com/books/making-the-baby
The Baby Battle (book 3)
https://ellisoday.com/books/the-baby-battle
Having the Baby (book 4)
https://ellisoday.com/books/having-the-baby

HOT HOLIDAYS
Hot Holidays -The Complete Series: Books 1-3
https://ellisoday.com/books/hot-holidays-books-1-3
The Mistletoe Game (Book 1) (free)
http://mybook.to/mistletoegame
A Banging New Year (Book 2)
https://ellisoday.com/books/a-banging-new-year
Cupid's Misfire (Book 3)

https://ellisoday.com/books/cupids-misfire

SIX NIGHTS OF SIN SERIES
Six Nights of Sin -The Complete Series: Books 1-6
https://ellisoday.com/books/six-nights-of-sin-books-1-6/

Interviewing For Her Lover (Book 1) **(Free)**
https://books2read.com/u/3nYKo6
Taking Control (Book 2)
https://ellisoday.com/books/taking-control
School Fantasy (Book 3)
https://ellisoday.com/books/school-fantasy
Master-Slave Fantasy (Book 4)
https://ellisoday.com/books/master-slave-fantasy
Punishment Fantasy (Book 5)
https://ellisoday.com/books/punishment-fantasy
The Proposition (Book 6)
https://ellisoday.com/books/the-proposition

THE VOYEUR SERIES
THE VOYEUR **(FREE)**
https://books2read.com/u/bxqBMk
Watching The Voyeur (Book 2)
https://ellisoday.com/books/watching-the-voyeur
Touching The Voyeur (Book 3)
https://ellisoday.com/books/touching-the-voyeur
Loving The Voyeur (Book 4)

https://ellisoday.com/books/loving-the-voyeur

The Voyeur Series (Books 1-4)
https://ellisoday.com/books/the-voyeur-series-books-1-4/

SIX WEEKS OF SEDUCTION
https://ellisoday.com/books/six-weeks-of-seduction

A MERRY MASQUERADE FOR CHRISTMAS
https://ellisoday.com/books/a-merry-masquerade-for-christmas/

THE DOM'S SUBMISSION SERIES
The Dom's Submission Box Set (Books 1-3)
https://ellisoday.com/books/the-doms-submission-books-1-3/
His Sub (Book 1) (**Free Ebook**)
https://books2read.com/u/3yrBlV
His Mission (Book 2)
https://ellisoday.com/books/his-mission/
His Submission (Book 3)
https://ellisoday.com/books/his-submission/

LA PETITE MORT CLUB INTIMATE ENCOUNTER SERIES
YOU KNOW THE PLAYERS, BUT DO YOU KNOW THE KINK?

HIS LESSON (TERRY AND MAGGIE)
https://ellisoday.com/books/his-lesson/

PLAYING HOUSE (NICK AND SARAH)
https://ellisoday.com/books/playing-house

HIS LOVE (TERRY AND MAGGIE)
https://ellisoday.com/books/his-love/

HIS IMPERFECT DAY (TERRY AND MAGGIE)
https://ellisoday.com/books/his-imperfect-day

COMING SOON:

ETHAN'S STORY

HARKER and ALISON'S STORY

MATTIE'S STORY

JAKE'S STORY

REBECCA AND DEREK'S STORY

VIC'S STORY

Email me with questions, concerns or to let me know what you thought of the book. I love hearing from readers.
authorEllisOday@gmail.com

https://www.EllisODay.com

Follow me

Facebook
https://www.facebook.com/EllisODayRomanceAuthor/

Closed FB Group (sneak peeks, sample chapters, and other bonuses)

Ellis O. Day

https://www.facebook.com/groups/153238782143373

Bookbub
https://www.bookbub.com/authors/Ellis-o-day

Instagram
https://www.instagram.com/authorEllisOday/

Twitter
https://twitter.com/Ellis_o_day

Pinterest
www.pinterest.com\AuthorEllisODay

ABOUT THE AUTHOR

Ellis O. Day loves reading and writing about love and sex. She believes that although the two don't have to go together, it's best when they do (both in life and in fantasy).

Ellis O. Day